Bestselling author Tori Carrington
introduces Private Scandals, a new miniseries
filled with lust, betrayal…and scandal like
you've never seen it!

When Troy, Ari and Bryna Metaxas realize
their business—and family—is on the brink
of ruin, how far will they go to save them?

Find out in…

Private Sessions
(October 2010)

Private Affairs
(November 2010)

Private Parts
(December 2010)

Blaze™

Dear Reader,

First loves, second chances... There's just something thrilling about this popular theme, isn't there? We thoroughly enjoyed revisiting it in this second book in our Private Scandals miniseries...stamping it, of course, with our own sizzling-hot brand!

In *Private Affairs*, sexy Palmer DeVoe returns to Earnest, Washington, a different man than he was years before. Only one thing remains the same—his bone-deep need for first love Penelope Weaver. And it appears absence only makes the sex grow hotter. Despite all the heartache Penelope has endured, Palmer is the one who introduced her to white-hot sex and heart-pounding love...and proves he's still more than capable of providing and stirring both. Her physical reaction to him gives her away every time their paths cross. But can she handle it if he leaves again...?

We hope you enjoy Palmer and Penelope's sizzling and sometimes heart-wrenching journey toward sexily-ever-after. We'd love to hear what you think. Contact us at P.O. Box 12271, Toledo, OH 43612 (we'll respond with a signed bookplate, newsletter and bookmark), or visit us on the web at www.toricarrington.net.

Here's wishing you love, romance and *hot* reading.

Lori & Tony Karayianni
aka Tori Carrington

Tori Carrington

PRIVATE AFFAIRS

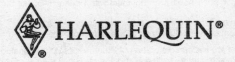

TORONTO • NEW YORK • LONDON
AMSTERDAM • PARIS • SYDNEY • HAMBURG
STOCKHOLM • ATHENS • TOKYO • MILAN • MADRID
PRAGUE • WARSAW • BUDAPEST • AUCKLAND

Recycling programs
for this product may
not exist in your area.

ISBN-13: 978-0-373-79578-9

PRIVATE AFFAIRS

Copyright © 2010 by Lori Karayianni & Tony Karayianni

ABOUT THE AUTHOR

Multi-award-winning, bestselling authors Lori Schlachter Karayianni and Tony Karayianni are the power behind the pen name Tori Carrington. Their more than forty-five titles include numerous Blaze miniseries, as well as the ongoing Sofie Metropolis comedic mystery series with another publisher. Visit www.toricarrington.net and www.sofiemetro.com for more information on the duo and their titles.

Books by Tori Carrington

Don't miss any of our special offers. Write to us at the following address for information on our newest releases.

Harlequin Reader Service
U.S.: 3010 Walden Ave., P.O. Box 1325, Buffalo, NY 14269
Canadian: P.O. Box 609, Fort Erie, Ont. L2A 5X3

We dedicate this book to our online friends
everywhere—you know who you are!

Interested in joining the fun? Check us out at
www.facebook.com/toricarrington or
www.twitter.com/toricarrington.

And, as always, to Brenda Chin,
a warm and wonderful constant
in an ever-changing world.

1

HOT. SO VERY HOT...

She lay against the picnic blanket and restlessly
watched as he fanned his hand across her trembling
belly, taking in her nakedness after he'd popped the
buttons down the front of her dress. The material glided
from her skin. She wasn't wearing a bra, which left him
to concentrate on the scrap of pink cotton that kept her
from being completely at the mercy of his hungry gaze.
He slid his thumbs under the thin straps at her hips,
slowly, ever so slowly, sliding her panties down until
she was finally free from them. She moved to close her
legs and he made a small sound of objection, instead
coaxing her to open to him. She wriggled as the summer
sun and his attention warmed her delicate flesh.

Then he was touching her...

Fingers stroked, probed, invaded, bringing her a plea-
sure that surely couldn't be real...

He leaned in, covering her mouth with his.

Too wet...too cloying...

She turned her head and he licked her ear instead.

No, no, she wanted to whisper. *Down...there...*

Penelope Weaver awakened with a start. Panting. Only it wasn't she who was out of breath. Or even the man that had been featured in her dream, as he was so often lately.

Instead, she stared at the blurry outline of her golden retriever/border collie mix and blanched away from his awful breath.

"Thor!"

Penelope sat up. It took a few moments to gather her wits about her. She wasn't lying on a picnic blanket in Old Man Benson's field just outside town, but was rather in her own bed in her room in the house on Maple Street. The summer sun cut a path across her body, but it was early evening and she was fully dressed.

And the too wet kiss hadn't come from her fantasy man, but rather her eight-year-old dog.

Bleech.

She picked up the wind-up alarm clock from the nightstand. Just after 7:00 p.m.

Just after seven!

Barnaby Jones would be there to pick her up any minute.

She sprung from the bed and rushed to the shared bathroom in the hall. She must have fallen asleep when she'd gone in to stretch out on the bed. It had been a long day at the small café she owned and ran on Main

Street and she'd needed to rest her feet for just a few moments.

The café. Even now it seemed odd to refer to her shop as such. She'd originally opened the place to sell her tapestries and called it Penelope's Possessions, but when the lumber mill had closed down four years ago it had taken much of what made downtown Earnest a draw for visitors with it. Businesses had closed, storefronts were empty. She'd adapted, offering her wares on the internet, but the shop itself had gradually become a coffee shop. Not a difficult transition seeing as she'd always made a good cup of coffee and thanks to her grandmother and great-aunt, there was an endless supply of baked goodies.

Now it was simply known as Penelope's.

She considered her curly dark hair in the mirror, fluffing the flattened back, and checking the liner around her brown eyes. Aside from a slight crease in her right cheek, she didn't look any the worse for wear. She took a deep breath and straightened the front of the dress she had on. A dress not unlike the one featured in her picnic dream. Only it really hadn't been a dream, had it? It was a memory. A recollection of a time that had passed long ago. Yet still had the power to steal her breath away.

She turned to hurry back out into the hall and nearly tripped over Thor.

"You're going to be the death of us both," she murmured, edging around him.

Of course, the reason he was shadowing her every

move was because there was no one else home to bother. The quiet was almost deafening. She walked into the living room, where the only sound was the hum of the laptop her grandmother had left on in the corner. The house's silence reminded her that the reason why no one was home was that the other inhabitants hoped she would get laid tonight.

Penelope groaned inwardly. Her grandmother and great-aunt were her roomies as well as two busybody, interfering old women whose sex lives were far more interesting than hers.

Interesting? That would require that she actually had a sex life to be *un*interesting. But she hadn't had one of those since...

She swallowed hard. Well, since around about the time of the dream she'd just had.

With quick jerks, she powered down the computer and closed the offending monitor, smoothing her hand over the top where it sat on an antique, accordion-front desk. From inkwells to laptops. There was a story in there somewhere. Perhaps on the different mediums meddling family members employed when trying to matchmake for younger family members.

It was summer in Earnest, Washington, and the sun wouldn't fully set for another two hours or so, but the mature trees that surrounded the quaint Victorian house filtered the light, making the house dim. She switched on a lamp and then moved back toward the hall and the kitchen, incapable of sitting to wait for the man who would arrive to take her out for their fifth date.

She frowned as she checked the dishwasher. Barnaby Jones wasn't so bad. He was even cute in a Vince Vaughn kind of way. Tall, broad-shouldered, easy going. But the town sheriff had yet to make her feel a twinge of what her dream had conjured up. There was a time or two when she'd actually orgasmed while asleep, the memories were so powerful.

Either that, or she was an inexcusably sorry individual.

At any rate, the good-night kiss Barnaby had given her at the end of the past two dates had left her feeling curiously…*sisterly* to him. And not in the Nietzsche way, either.

She hated to break it to her grandma Agatha and her great-aunt Irene, but there wasn't going to be any sex had in this house tonight, no matter how quiet and available.

She did appreciate the clean set of sheets Aggie had put on her bed in preparation for "the big event," however. The fresh scent of line-dried cotton was likely responsible for her drifting off.

As for the dream…

Well, she wasn't going to think about that now. Or connect the current frequency of them to the fact that the man in question had been spotted back in town. And forget his possible nearness having anything to do with her mixed feelings about Barnaby. She hadn't seen him in nearly fifteen years. He no longer influenced anything she did or thought or felt.

Thor whined at her feet.

Penelope twisted her lips. "What is it, boy? You have water. Food…"

Probably he wanted to go outside.

She glanced at her watch. It wasn't such a bad idea. She could check her roses and the vegetable garden while she was out there with him.

She opened the back screen door with a muted squeak and Thor bounded out, her following on his heels. The door clapped shut and she stood looking at a garden that had changed very little in the thirty years she'd lived there. Oh, the trees might have grown a little taller, and the wooden privacy fence at the back of the property was only a few years old. But the same perennials dotted the landscape, the vegetable garden was in the same spot as it always was. And the enclosed, intimate gazebo at the far end of the yard was exactly the same but for a couple of coats of white paint.

She found herself drawn to the structure in which she'd spent so much of her teenaged years, bypassing her roses and not stopping until she stood in the arch looking in at the overstuffed cushions that had supported her while she read countless books…and had also been the setting for many of her dreams.

Her hand went to the side of her neck, feeling oddly exposed at that one moment. It was almost as if someone was watching her.

"Hello, Penelope."

She swiveled so quickly she nearly lost her footing on the wooden steps.

And Palmer DeVoe reached out to steady her...

BEAUTIFUL...

No matter how many times Palmer had anticipated this moment, this particular point in time when he'd finally come face to face with Penelope Weaver after so many years, he could never have imagined the completely visceral feelings that would roll through him like a thousand rippling Pacific waves. Need, want, fear emerged one by one, then were washed away by the next emotion.

In his mind's eye, Penelope was still the fresh-faced young woman with the warm smile and deep dimples and slender body. His first sexual encounter, his high school sweetheart, and yes, he admitted, his first love.

Now she was an earthy, sexy, curvy woman who somehow reached even deeper inside him, searching for something he was afraid wasn't there for her to find.

Her curly hair was a little shorter. Her face a little fuller. But her smile was just as warm. Her dark eyes just as probing.

Palmer still held her arm where he'd steadied her. They both looked down at where their skin connected. He lingered a bit longer, marveling at her softness.

Then, as if by mutual agreement, he removed

his hand and she stepped beyond his grasp at the same time.

"I heard you were in town," she said quietly.

Rarely in his memories of her did she speak. Instead, her image was like a series of snapshots of her in various poses, most of them under him.

Now, her voice flowed over him, intoxicating.

He nodded toward the gazebo behind her. "Now that's a familiar place."

She glanced over her shoulder and blushed. If he didn't know better, he'd think that she'd been thinking about him, about them, when he'd walked up.

He hadn't planned to stop; he'd merely been walking by—as he'd had on several prior occasions—when he'd spotted her standing there like a ghost from the past.

Penelope moved through the yard toward the back door of the house and he watched her go, the material of her dress hugging her in all the right places.

He'd known running into her at some point was inevitable. While he'd visited his hometown a couple of times in recent weeks, he was now living here. At least for the foreseeable future. Which meant facing a great number of people from his past.

"This isn't a good time, Palmer," she said quietly.

He squinted at her through the waning light. "I would have called, but…"

A sad attempt at humor that fell flat on its face, where it belonged.

He cleared his throat. "I hadn't meant to stop. I was

walking back from Main on my way to Foss's bed-and-breakfast…"

She nodded. "I guessed as much."

She looked at him in a way that made him feel she was sizing him up and that he came up short.

"You look good, Palmer," she said simply.

"So do you."

Her smile was self-conscious. "I don't mean…physically." She made a small sound. "It looks like you've done well for yourself."

And he had, hadn't he? He'd accomplished everything that he'd hoped to when he left Earnest for Boston. More.

Why was it, then, that he suddenly sensed he'd achieved nothing?

"Hello?" a man's voice called from inside the house.

Penelope looked in that direction, apparently surprised.

Palmer grimaced. While he hadn't asked for the information, many townspeople that he'd encountered seemed to deem it important to fill him in on Penelope and her actions. He'd learned that she was still single. That she owned a small shop down on Main, one of the few that had managed to stay open in the struggling town of four thousand. He'd walked by it a few times after closing and had stood staring inside at the colorful tapestries on the walls and displayed on easels.

In all the conversations he'd had, not a one of them had mentioned a man being in the picture.

But of course there would be. Why would he even think differently?

"Have you visited your father yet?" she asked, speaking to him rather than the man seeking her out.

He suspected she knew the answer to that. Just as he knew many secondhand details about her, she'd probably plucked the details of his movements since he'd been back from the same grapevine. Not that it was a state secret, but he was pretty sure that everyone knew he had yet to see his old man.

The back door opened and a familiar guy walked out. A guy who towered over him by several inches and had made it his business to stop by the industrial trailer that currently served as his offices. Sheriff Barnaby Jones had let him know in no uncertain terms that he intended to keep an eye on what was going on.

At the time, Palmer couldn't help sensing that there was a certain trace of animosity in the sheriff's attention.

Now he knew why.

Penelope hurried toward the man. "Barney! Hi."

The sheriff's gaze seemed a little too intimate for Palmer's liking as he took in Penelope and complimented her on her dress. Then his attention fell on Palmer where he stood just inside the side garden gate. His expression changed.

"Barnaby, I'd like to introduce you to...an old family

friend," Penelope said. "Palmer DeVoe, this is Barnaby Jones."

Palmer crossed to shake the other man's hand. "I believe we've already met."

"Yes, we have." The sheriff seemed to say it in warning.

Penelope appeared to pick up on the undercurrents passing between them and stepped in.

"Barney and I are attending the fair in Lewisville," she said, and then looked confused, as if she couldn't understand why she'd shared that. "It was...nice to see you, Palmer. I hope you enjoy your visit. You haven't been home for a while and I know everyone is happy to see you."

Palmer squared his shoulders under the scrutiny of the sheriff and turned a full-wattage grin on Penelope. "Visit? I'm not visiting, Penelope. I'm back."

2

THE INACCURATE COMMENT had earned exactly the response Palmer was looking for. But that meant little when Penelope had walked inside the house with Barnaby, leaving him alone to see himself back out the garden gate.

"And remember, no matter where you go, there you are."

The quote from Confucius that his mother had liked to parrot trailed through his mind as he walked toward the B and B. He slid his hands into the pockets of his khaki pants, considering the words of the other woman he had loved and lost. But this time to death.

Janice DeVoe had been so sweet that his father had once remarked that a body didn't need sugar in his coffee when she was in the room. Of course, that had been long before things had turned sour. And before she'd gotten sick with an illness that she'd denied until it was too late.

She'd been fond of telling stories about her only child, the unchallenged sunshine of her life, of how he proclaimed nearly from the instant he could speak that he was going to be someone important, the richest man in the world and, if he could fit it in, president. And she'd encouraged him in whatever direction he wanted to go.

Until she lay near death, considering the son she'd loved so dearly…and the father that had initially been amused by the special mother-and-son bond, and then increasingly jealous of it.

That's when Janice had spoken the quote one last time, calling on both of the men in her life to reconcile their differences and come together. Told them they would need each other now.

Then she was gone and he and his father had stared at each other, virtual strangers.

Shortly thereafter, Palmer had left. And aside from brief phone calls around the holidays and on birthdays, they'd barely spoken since.

Now, Palmer neared the corner of Maple and Elm streets and he stopped before crossing. Not because of traffic. There was none at this time on a Friday night. But because instead of walking straight toward the B and B he could turn right and within three blocks be on the street on which he'd grown up and had not been back to since he was nineteen.

"I'll be in the area next week," he'd said to his father during a recent phone call.

Thomas had made a sound. "I'll alert the media."

There had been no invitation to visit. No indication that he'd like to see him. Just a sarcastic remark that Palmer had left hanging in the air between them.

Before he knew that's what he was going to do, he made that right and took the route he had taken so very many times before. Within minutes he stood in front of the house his mother had taken such pride in. A place he might not have recognized if not for the tilting, rusty mailbox at the unpaved curb that bore the family name.

The simple, one-story clapboard house had at one time been painted a brilliant white with powder-blue shutters. The flower beds had been full of color, the shrubs neatly trimmed, the grass mown. Now everything looked abandoned, as if the only owner had been his mother and no one had lived there since.

Palmer opened the gate that hung half off its hinges and stepped slowly up the weed-choked gravel path. The shrubs had grown unevenly to nearly halfway up the front windows and a newspaper sat on the cracked concrete front steps. He picked it up, verifying that it was today's, and then leaned forward to knock. The screen door was so grimy that he hadn't noticed the front door was actually open until he heard his old man's gravelly voice as clearly as if he were standing next to him.

"What the hell do you want?" he called. "If you're selling something, I ain't buying."

More words followed but they were said quietly and

apparently not meant for whatever visitor stood outside the door.

How easy it would be just to turn away. To leave and pretend he'd never visited.

Palmer reached for the door handle only to find it was locked.

"I asked what in the hell you want."

The old man stood directly on the other side of the screen door now, staring out at him.

Thomas DeVoe didn't recognize him.

And Palmer wouldn't have recognized him if not for the fact that he knew he was at the right house.

While his father had been tall, he seemed to have shrunk a few inches. Or maybe it was the way his shoulders curved forward as if unable to hold himself completely upright anymore. The three-day stubble on his face made it look even more haggard than it probably was, and his graying hair spoke of the fact that he was at least a month late for a visit to the barber's. He wore a tank T-shirt that was more gray than white and his slacks would have fallen from his thin hips if not for the belt pulled tightly around them.

Palmer lifted the paper to wave at him. "Hi, Pops."

Thomas squinted at him, the stench of liquor seeming to emanate from his every pore.

"I only have one son and you're not him," he said, and then reached to close the door.

No matter where you go, there you are...

"ARE YOU ALL RIGHT?" Barnaby asked Penelope for the third time in an hour.

Penelope slid her hand into the crook of his arm as they walked the fair paths, the scent of corn dogs and cotton candy filling the air along with the happy shrieks of children enjoying the carnival rides.

"I'm fine," she assured him.

Which was a bald-faced lie. She wasn't fine. Her mind was still on the scene in the backyard before her date had arrived. And her body still hummed as if Palmer had touched her with more than his gaze.

She suspected the dream she'd had before encountering him hadn't helped. But it was more than that. Putting together the Palmer of her past with the man of the present hadn't been nearly as difficult as she'd thought it might be.

So many people she'd attended high school with had changed dramatically. Facial features had broadened or narrowed, grown fuller or thinner, some so much so that she often didn't recognize them. Not Palmer. She could have picked him out instantly. Even in a crowd like tonight's, her gaze would have immediately homed in on the man who was even more attractive now than he had been then.

Damn him.

"Would you like an elephant ear?" Barnaby asked.

Penelope squinted at him. "Pardon me?"

He pointed to a nearby food booth.

She laughed quietly in understanding, then looked down at where she absently rubbed her abdomen. She already felt as if she had a real elephant ear in her stomach and it was furiously trying to flap its way out.

"Are you sure you're all right?"

Penelope faltered. "I'm sorry," she said with genuine affection. "But I guess I'm not. I must have eaten something earlier that didn't agree with me..."

"The corn dog?"

"I don't think so. This goes to before we got here."

Began the instant she looked into Palmer's eyes.

"I really hate to ask, but do you think you can take me home?"

He searched her face, but if there was any answer to be had there, apparently he didn't find it. "That bad?"

She nodded. "I really hate to ruin the night, but all I can think about is going home and lying down."

And flipping through the scrapbook of her memories.

Of course, she didn't tell him that. Would never admit that Palmer's appearance had had such an unexpected impact on her. Not to Barnaby. Not to anyone.

So much of what had transpired between her and Palmer had been unbearably private. There had really been no one to talk to back then. Or now.

Should she take it into her head to mention the visit to her grandmother, she could just imagine the reaction. The frowns. The head-shaking. The questions.

"Would you like one to go?" Barnaby asked.

She smiled. "Yes, yes. That would be nice. Thank you."

PENELOPE STOOD ON THE FRONT PORCH, a wrapped elephant ear in her hands as she faced Barnaby.

"Would you like me to come in?" he asked.

She looked down. Well, that was a first. Usually Barnaby was comfortable allowing her to set the tone. She shook her head. "No. I'm afraid I wouldn't be very good company."

Night had fallen, day little more than a purple smear against the western sky. She'd left the porch light on and it threw Barnaby's handsome features into soft relief.

"Thank you for taking me to the fair. And for this." She lifted the sweet.

"You're welcome, Penelope."

He moved up the last step. She knew he was preparing to kiss her and she mentally scrambled for a way to avoid the awkward meeting.

"Goodnight, Barnaby," she said and turned. "I really must take something for this upset stomach."

"A soda always works wonders for me," he said.

She quickly unlocked the door and went inside. "Thanks. That may be exactly what I need."

Before he could offer to get one for her, she closed the door with a clap and then stood for long moments, listening for sounds that he was leaving. Realizing that he might be waiting to see that she was safe inside, she leaned over to switch on a lamp, and then peered through the curtains. He still stood where she'd left him.

She gave a little wave and then closed the door curtains again.

Finally, she heard the sound of his footfalls as he walked back to his car, and then the crank of his truck engine.

Penelope let out a long sigh, unaware that she'd been holding her breath.

She stepped toward the kitchen, flipping on lights as she went. It wasn't fair, really. On paper, Barnaby Jones was the perfect man for her. Beyond being great looking and single, they'd attended the same schools, knew all the same people, and enjoyed doing the same things.

Maybe that was the problem: they were too well matched.

She put the elephant ear down on the counter, inwardly cursing her meddling grandmother and aunt.

Of course, Barnaby was worlds better than some of the other men they'd fixed her up with. There had been the divorced car mechanic who'd liked to flex his muscles for her expected enjoyment every five minutes. And the nerdy bank vice president who pushed his glasses up constantly and rarely met her gaze, and then grabbed onto her so tightly when she'd kissed him good-night that she'd been half afraid he wouldn't let go. She'd nearly pushed him down the stairs just to get him to disconnect.

So on the date scale, Barnaby was the best match yet.

If only kissing him wasn't like kissing her grandmother.

She made a face at the comparison and then realized that the house was too quiet. And it wasn't just the absence of the two old biddies who had gotten her into her current mess either.

"Thor?" she called out.

No response. Which wasn't all that unusual. If he was curled up sleepy somewhere, he'd likely stay exactly where he was.

She opened the pantry door and took out the bag of his favorite dog treats. Still no Thor.

That was odd. By now he would be panting at her feet.

She shook the bag. "Who's been a good boy?" she called out in a lilting tone. "Who thinks they're deserving of a goodie?" She shook the bag again.

Nothing.

Huh.

Then it dawned on her that she might have left him out back.

She unlocked the door and pulled it open. Nothing. She flicked on the back light.

"Thor?" she called into the night.

A single bark somewhere in the yard.

She grimaced and stepped onto the back porch. *Please don't let him have cornered another badger. Or, worse, another skunk.* She'd bathed him three times, once in tomato juice, another in lemon juice, but nothing but time had seemed capable of ridding him of the god-awful stench. They'd kept him locked outside for two miserable days with him whining the whole night through.

"Thor, come here," she ordered, giving an experimental sniff. Nothing but the fragrant scent of her rosebushes.

Another quiet bark.

Penelope navigated the stairs and walked up the pathway. She heard his panting before she saw him. Or, rather, saw his tail wagging where he sat inside the gazebo.

"What are you doing there?" she asked, coming up behind him.

He turned and licked her outstretched hand, then sniffed animatedly at the bag she still held.

"I have half a mind not to give you a treat because I don't think you've been a very good boy."

His tail was now little more than a blur as he picked up wagging speed and began doing his crouch and bark and run in circles treat-dance.

She laughed. "Oh, all right. Maybe just one."

A shadow moved in the gazebo. "How about this bad boy?" a familiar voice asked. "Do you think he's entitled to any treats?"

3

PALMER HADN'T EXPECTED her to return so soon. Had even feared she might not be alone when she did. But here she was, and there was no suspicious sheriff in tow. Which made him much luckier than he'd been earlier in the evening when he'd paid his surprise visit to his father.

"Palmer!" she whispered. "What are you doing in there?"

He grimaced. What was he doing in there, indeed? "Sitting." He went for the obvious.

There was a long silence as the summer night sounds penetrated the thin walls of the gazebo. The structure smelled of wood and flowers, the cushions on the bench soft and accommodating.

How many times had the two of them met secretly in this very place, concealed by the shadows? A dozen times? A dozen dozen?

"Have you been here since I left?"

"No."

Although he wished differently. His father's reaction had hit him hard. Harder than he would have imagined it might. What man turned his own blood away from the door? Especially considering that man didn't appear to have anyone else.

To his surprise, Penelope came inside the gazebo and sat opposite him. She was little more than a warm blur and quiet breathing, the subtle scent of jasmine tempting his thoughts...elsewhere.

"That was a short date," he commented.

He heard her soft laugh. "Yes. It was."

"I hope I didn't ruin things."

She shifted, leaning back against the cushions. "Why is it that I doubt that?"

"Maybe because you always did know me better than I gave you credit for."

He heard her swallow. "Not as well as I'd hoped, it appears."

The words were said so quietly he nearly didn't hear them.

While years separated tonight from the last time they'd shared the gazebo, it seemed as if it could have been yesterday. Not because of what he said, or she did. But because of the way he felt.

Palmer planted his forearms on his thighs and joined his hands between his knees. The movement put him within touching distance of Penelope. He waited to see if she'd move away or stay put. He knew a little thrill when she stayed put.

It was odd, the...need he felt for her. Even now. Time and space and maturity had made him believe that what he remembered was kid stuff. A major crush. A hormonally induced love.

But that theory no longer held water. Because right now he felt just as needy as he had back then. Perhaps even more so. All he wanted to do was reach over and haul her into his lap. Claim that mouth of hers with his. Lay his hand against her soft breast. Hear her sigh in his ear.

He cleared his throat. "I went to visit my father tonight."

He swore he could feel her gaze probing his face in the dark.

"I know I should have gone before now... He'd heard I was back..."

He ran his hands through his hair and then returned to clutching them between his knees.

"He pretended not to know me and closed the door."

She made a small sound he interpreted as surprise.

Palmer squinted in her direction although he couldn't really see her. "Is it possible that he didn't recognize his own blood?"

Penelope knew of his awkward at best, animosity-filled at worst, relationship with his father going way back. In fact, she was the only one who'd known outside his own mother. He'd told her all about it. Well, not everything.

"I knew who you were instantly," she whispered.

Thank God for that, he thought. He didn't know what he would have done had he faced rejection twice in one night.

Then again, if it weren't for Penelope's suggestion that he see his father, he might never have gone over there.

"So why do you think he did it?" he asked.

She made another small sound, but this time not because of what he'd said, but because he'd stretched his fingers and the tips were touching her knees. The hem of her dress fell just above, leaving him free to feel her warm skin.

And she *was* warm… And soft… And inviting…

God help him, but he wanted her so badly he hurt.

"Palmer…please…"

His hands drifted upward as if on their own accord, tunneling under the material.

Penelope gasped and trapped them with hers.

He was close enough to kiss her. Close enough to smell her skin. Close enough to feel her breath against his face.

"When I first saw you tonight," he whispered, his voice ragged, "I thought I'd traveled back in time. Back to when we were both kids. When the world was nothing but a big question mark outside that gate. And where nothing existed but my need to kiss you."

He was surprised by his words. It was one thing to

privately acknowledge them. Another to put them out there where she might rebuff them. Might rebuff him.

"When I agreed to come back here to see to this business venture...I'd hoped I might see you." Her hands were still on his. "But I never expected to feel this... way for you. Again."

He closed his eyes and swallowed hard.

"I understand that you may not feel the same..."

Long heartbeats passed. Palmer didn't speak. And neither did Penelope. They merely sat there practically forehead-to-forehead, him with his eyes closed.

Then, finally, she spoke.

"That's the problem." She paused. "I feel exactly the same..."

AND IT WAS A PROBLEM for Penelope. A monumental dilemma. Because whereas Palmer seemed glad to be feeling the way he had way back then, she was heartbroken to find herself in a place she never expected to be again.

So much time had passed...

Yet it amounted to a little more than a drop in a bucket...

She tried to think of Barnaby. To hold desperately onto all of the reasons why she shouldn't let Palmer kiss her. But as he leaned even closer to her, all reason fled, leaving only acute awareness in its wake.

When his lips finally met hers, a moan years in the making wound up and around her throat, exiting softly.

She released his hands and snaked her arms over his shoulders. How could he taste the same? How could his hair still be thick and coarse against her fingers? How could that longing that she hadn't experienced since he'd left emerge as if he had never disappeared?

Palmer groaned, his freed hands sliding even further up under her dress. When the back of his fingers skimmed the front of her damp panties, she nearly jumped from the seat.

"God, I'd forgotten how responsive you were." He kissed her long and hard. "I could always count on knowing exactly how you felt about me, Penelope. That you wanted me as much as I wanted you."

She bit her bottom lip, hating the hot tears that flooded her eyes.

That's not true, she wanted to say. *If you'd wanted me as much as I'd wanted you, you would never have left.*

But before she could truly consider the weight of her words, he was shifting her weight from the other side of the gazebo to across his lap. Penelope gasped and held onto his shoulders for balance, surprised by the move. Before she could regain her balance both physically and emotionally, he cupped the side of her face, holding her still while he launched a fresh assault on her trembling mouth.

Having him this close, his heat permeating her every cell, his chest against her side, his lap under her bottom, it was impossible to think about anything beyond her growing need. As his breathing grew more ragged, hers did, too. And her hands seemed to have taken on a life of their own. They tunneled into his hair, dove down his back, exploring the long, hard length, then circled to press against the hard wall of his chest. He felt good. Solid. A far sight better than what she'd experienced in her dreams. He was there. Present. And she intended to take every advantage of that fact.

Shifting around, she straddled him, adjusting her skirt so that the only things separating them were the thin wall of her panties and his slacks.

She stilled. Not because she knew a moment of hesitancy. But because she cherished the white hot heat flashing through her.

She'd forgotten what it felt like to think nothing at all. To give herself over to sheer emotion. To surrender to something that was bigger than her.

"Christ, you're even more beautiful now than you were then," Palmer murmured.

Penelope pressed a finger against his lips. "Shh. Please. Don't speak…"

At least not with words. She wanted him to communicate with his body. Wanted him to touch her. Everywhere.

And he did.

Penelope gasped when he fanned his hands against her bottom and then budged them ever so slowly downward until his fingers were under the hem of her bunched up dress. Skin met skin, sending shivers down her back, causing her to arch her body, seeking a more intimate meeting.

And he gave it to her…

His fingers burrowed under the elastic of her panties and cupped her bottom. Then his fingertips followed the shallow crevice inward until they pressed against her swollen folds.

Penelope tugged her mouth away from his, breathing heavily against his cheek as his fingers found their target.

Yes…

She heard Palmer mumble something then curse.

"I don't have protection," he said into her ear.

Penelope's throat refused the swallow she tried to force down it, his words too familiar.

She went still for long moments, trying to gather her scattered emotions into some sort of order. Then she slowly drew away from him, forcing him to release his hold on her both literally and figuratively. Moments later, she sat with her legs tightly closed, her dress back in place, next to him.

"I wasn't expecting…this," he said quietly.

Neither had she. Not that she usually traveled with condoms anyway. But it was somewhat reassuring that he hadn't whipped a ready one out of his back pocket.

Reassuring and disquieting.

He skimmed the back of his knuckles along her jaw and kissed her again, long and hard, stretching open the gulf of sensation that she was trying desperately to close.

He cursed once more.

She smiled.

"Tell me we'll be here again, Penelope." He stared into her eyes.

She looked away and bit hard on her bottom lip, unable to answer.

"I didn't expect to be here now," she whispered.

He drew away and sat back against the cushions. "That sounds a little too much like a no to me."

"No," she said. "It sounds like a maybe."

4

"SHH, YOU'LL WAKE HER."

"Shush, yourself. You're the one making all the noise."

Penelope easily identified the two voices coming from her open bedroom door even as she fought to hold onto sleep. She'd gotten so little of it. Hadn't she just finally dropped off? She pried open one eye and read the clock. After eight a.m. The last time she'd looked, it had been after four. And her mind had still been racing with images from the night before. Her ears still filled with the sounds. Her body still reeling from the shock of emotions.

"Can you tell whether or not he was in there with her?" Her grandmother's stage whisper was louder than her regular speaking voice. It was a well-known fact, but no one seemed to have the heart to tell her.

"How would I know?" her great-aunt asked, just slightly quieter.

"Come on, let's go before she wakes up."

Penelope rolled over and eyed the two busybodies who were also her roommates. "Too late."

Her grandmother made a face even as she sharply elbowed Irene. "I told you you'd wake her."

Her aunt gave her a long look and then entered the room fully. "That's all right. Now that she's up, we can ask her."

Penelope's right arm was still curled around the guest pillow on the double bed. Her great-aunt tugged it from her grip and gave it a thorough inspection.

"What are you looking for?" Penelope rose up on her elbows.

Irene plucked at something and then held up what appeared to be a single hair. She frowned. "What color is his hair?"

"Blond."

"This is dark."

Penelope gave an exasperated eye roll. "Probably it's Thor's."

Her aunt sighed and then dropped the hair, brushing her hands together.

"Well, whose did you expect it to be?" Penelope asked with a raised brow.

Her grandmother came up the other side of the bed. "Don't play coy with me, little girl. You know perfectly well who. I changed the sheets yesterday special for the occasion." She considered Penelope through narrow eyes. "The question is, did you make good use of them?"

Penelope swung her legs over the side of the bed and sat up. It was far too early for this. "Of course, I made good use of them. I slept on them."

She dragged her robe from where it lay over the wicker chair in the corner and put it on, weaving her way around the two old women planted in her room. Unsurprisingly, they gave chase, following her to the kitchen where she took a cup out of the cabinet and poured a hefty dose of coffee from the maker.

"So we went to Seattle for nothing, then," her aunt said with a deep sigh.

Penelope remembered what had transpired in the gazebo and silently told them they hadn't wasted a minute. She took a deep sip of coffee, only to nearly spit it out.

"What is this?" she asked, wiping her mouth with the back of her hand.

Her grandmother smiled. "Gourmet stuff we picked up last night. Double chocolate mocha almond amaretto something or other. What, don't you like it?"

Penelope poured the cup's contents down the drain.

"Hey, that cost four times what our regular stuff does," her aunt complained.

"Yes, well, then you got ripped off."

To Penelope, coffee was coffee, straight, no special flavorings or additions or fancy names. Good ole Juan

Valdez beans freshly brewed was all she desired and needed.

Funny that emotionally she went for the complicated stuff.

She grimaced and put a cup of water in the microwave and nuked it so she could have some green tea instead. Plain. No lemon or honey. Just simple green tea.

She sat at the table, dipping the bag into the steamy water.

"Who drinks hot tea in the summer?" her great-aunt asked, putting a plate of muffins on the table.

"How is it different than drinking hot coffee?" her grandmother wanted to know, sitting down.

Penelope ignored them as she squeezed the liquid from the bag and put it on the table. She took a long sip. That was more like it.

Finally, she looked up to find Agatha and Irene staring at her.

"What?" she asked, and then groaned. "Not that again."

"And again and again and again," her grandmother promised. "Penny, girl, you need to get laid."

Her aunt nodded her head several times, barely disturbing her tight gray curls. "Yes, you do."

"But how are you going to do that if you keep your thighs glued together?"

Penelope gasped and quickly raised her hand to ward them off. "Please, don't. It's much too early in the morning for me to contemplate talking about sex with my grandmother and great-aunt."

"Well, you should have thought about that last night. If you had done what you were supposed to, we wouldn't have to talk about it at all."

Penelope narrowed her eyes. "Hmm. Somehow I doubt that." She put her cup down on the table. "I get the feeling that you two would want detailed descriptions."

"God, girl, why would we want those?"

Her aunt put a muffin on a napkin and pushed it toward her. "We have sex lives. You don't." She waggled a brow. "Now if *you* should want details…"

"Oh, God, please. Spare me."

"Couldn't hurt," her grandmother said. "Maybe it will remind her what she's missing."

"And maybe the images you burn into my brain will scar me for life, and leave me unable to ever have sex again."

Both their mouths closed with a snap.

That was better. Much better.

Penelope ignored the muffin and enjoyed her tea.

It was hard to imagine a time when she didn't have these two feisty, witty women in her life. In fact, very little had changed since she was five and her own mother had taken off for parts unknown with her latest boyfriend, an occasional visit or phone call to let them know she was still alive Penelope's only contact with the woman who had birthed her.

Agatha and Irene had raised her, although at times

it had been difficult to tell who was the child and who the adults. While there had always been freshly baked and cooked food in the house, so had there been parties and a seemingly never-ending trail of paramours, the reputation of the two sisters in their younger years following them well into the autumn of their lives. More often than not it had been Penelope who had picked up beer bottles from the floor and cigarette butts from the plants after a particularly rowdy night.

She had hoped that one day they would settle down. That her grandmother and great-aunt would finally mature. But it appeared that might not ever happen.

"So how was Seattle?" she asked, idly pulling apart the muffin and popping a piece into her mouth.

The two sisters grinned at each other. And Penelope sat back, readying herself for another example of exactly why neither of them would ever qualify for a spot in a Norman Rockwell painting...

PALMER STOOD AT THE FRONT DESK at Foss's B and B and stared at the bell after looking at his watch. The scent of fresh coffee and something baking came from the direction of the kitchen, but seeing as he was the only guest in the seven-room inn, he didn't feel comfortable just walking around the place as if he owned it. Especially since from the moment he'd checked in, he'd gotten the impression he wasn't exactly welcome. The second afternoon of his stay, he'd returned to find his suitcase on the front porch, his room locked up.

"I didn't realize you were staying for more than one night," Debra Foss had said when he'd finally tracked her down in the back garden.

He knew differently. He'd told her when he'd checked in to what basically amounted to the only temporary accommodations in town, that he would be staying indefinitely.

But he hadn't bothered to remind her. He could tell by the look on her face that she understood what the score was, and nothing he could say would sway her.

So he made it a point of stopping by the front desk to reinstate his intention to stay and pay for another night before leaving for the day, lest he return to find his suitcase in a garbage can.

He rang the bell.

He wasn't altogether sure why he'd received the cold shoulder upon his return to his hometown. He certainly hadn't left on bad terms with anyone. Well, outside of his father, anyway. So why the cold reception?

Mrs. Foss popped up behind the desk, startling him. She didn't wish him a good morning or offer him a cup of coffee, she merely accepted his money, showed him where to sign—again—and then disappeared to wherever she'd emerged from.

Not the best way to start the day.

Palmer stepped out into the summer morning, blinking against the strong sunlight. He couldn't remember it being this hot here. Many summers it had barely gotten warm enough to set up the sprinkler in the back yard, yet now his shirt immediately stuck to his back, and he wanted to loosen the tie he'd just tightened.

He walked across the arched gravel drive and unlocked the door to his leased Mercedes, draping his suit jacket over the back of the driver's chair before getting in and starting the engine, counting to ten as he waited for the air conditioner to kick in.

Ah, yes. That was more like it.

He understood the entire state was experiencing a fluke heat wave unlike any they'd seen before. Up in Seattle, the temperature had broken a hundred for the first time in…well, recorded history. And it hadn't rained in at least a couple of weeks, which was strange in and of itself.

The thought brought the image of Penelope in the gazebo last night to mind. She'd smelled of summer and made him hot just looking at her.

Palmer rubbed the back of his neck. The last thing he'd planned was trying to seduce her in the backyard of her grandmother's house. But there you had it. Seemed the more things changed, the more they stayed the same. He wanted her even more than he had back then. Then again, perhaps time had dulled the old memories. And now reality had honed them to an aching point.

He couldn't help looking around Earnest as he drove through the few blocks that comprised the downtown on his way south to the construction site he'd chosen. It held little more than the trailer that served as his offices for the time being.

He eased his foot up off the gas, spotting someone walking across Main Street.

Penelope.

He stopped altogether.

She was wearing another dress, this time tan with what appeared to be—were those cherries?—printed all over the light material. A wide-brimmed hat protected her dark head from the morning sun and she reached up to steady it as a breeze threatened to take it from her.

A car horn beeped behind him. Penelope looked over her shoulder in his direction.

Palmer grimaced and gave a brief wave. "Hey, how are you doing? Me? I'm pissed my discreet moment of watching you was so rudely interrupted."

He glanced in the mirror to see who the perpetrator was. Why wasn't he surprised to find Barnaby in his sheriff's car?

He flashed the red-and-white strobe lights on top of his official county vehicle.

Palmer gave him a wave, as well, rather than the finger he would like to have flashed, and put the car back in gear, the moment broken.

Within five minutes, he turned into the narrow un-paved road that led to the trailer. A pickup kicked up dust as it raced toward him at high speed.

What the hell?

At the last moment, Palmer pulled into the brush and the pickup roared by, momentarily blinding him with the dirt cloud it left behind.

If he hadn't felt unwelcome before, that little stunt certainly would have clued him in.

He continued on to the trailer and got out, walking toward the construction foreman he'd hired the week before.

"Morning," he said, shaking John Nelson's hand. "What was all that about?"

"You tell me."

Palmer squinted at him. "Excuse me?"

"If you had waited a minute longer, it would have been me coming at you head-on on that road." John slapped a file he was holding against his chest. "And I wouldn't have missed."

He began stalking toward his own truck.

"Hey, what's up, man?" Palmer asked, grabbing his arm to stop him.

"You might want to try asking the man in there." John jabbed a thumb toward the trailer. "He just fired us all."

5

"GOOD MORNING, PENELOPE."

Penelope looked up from where she was fiddling with the espresso machine and found the sheriff standing in the open doorway, his hat in his hands.

"Hey, Barnaby," she said.

She closed the appliance door and pressed the button for brew, pretending everything was as they'd left it last night at the door to her grandmother's house.

Only it wasn't, was it? Everything had changed.

She cleared her throat and wiped down the counter although she'd already cleaned it.

"Everything all right?"

She glanced up to find Barnaby standing on the other side of the counter, a concerned expression on his handsome face.

She tried for a smile. "Everything's fine. Why do you ask?"

"That Palmer DeVoe character hasn't been giving you any trouble?"

She nearly laughed. Instead, she cleared her throat again. "No. Of course, not."

But he was, wasn't he? The instant Palmer DeVoe had driven back into town her life had been in utter chaos. Because she'd known at some point that their paths would cross. And all those old emotions would surface.

Only she'd had no idea they would burn so hot. So strong.

"The usual?" she asked.

Barnaby nodded. "Do you have any of those blueberry muffins your grandmother makes?"

"Of course. One or two?"

"Actually, I was thinking of taking some back to the station. So you'd better make it an even dozen."

Penelope filled the travel cup he produced with vanilla roast coffee and then constructed a carton. "You know, you don't have to keep doing this, Barnaby."

"Doing what?"

"Coming by here every morning in order to throw some business my way."

His grin was quick and bright.

"I mean, I appreciate it, but I'm okay until things start turning around here."

"You think my morning visits are for charity purposes?"

She squinted at him. "Aren't they?"

"And if I told you I come by to see you because my day goes better if I do?"

She put the muffins inside the box. "Then you don't have to pay anything for that."

He accepted his cup and the box. "And if I happen to like the coffee and the muffins?"

She leaned against the counter. "Then I'd say I hope to see you back here tomorrow."

His chuckle was full and genuine. And she responded in kind.

Barnaby Jones was a great guy. He'd been a couple of years ahead of her in school. She'd known him not only because he'd been the star basketball player, but because he'd been half of an infamous couple: Barnaby and Barbara. One didn't say one name without saying the other.

As was the case with most high school sweethearts, when they graduated, the two had married.

As was not the case with most high school sweethearts, after ten childless years, they divorced...and Barbie entered into a lesbian relationship with the local librarian, both of them living in an apartment over the diner across the street.

Of course, the town still buzzed with gossip every time one or the other of the former couple was spotted. "That poor Barnaby" was usually said about him. And "that Barbie woman" was usually said about her.

Penelope knew them both. And understood that there was no bad blood between them. They even got together for dinner once a month at the pub or diner, acting like old friends. Which was probably what they had been, even before they got married.

Penelope had asked Barbara once why she'd married Barnaby if she'd known she was gay. Her answer had been that there hadn't been any other options. Until the librarian had moved to town, that is.

Now, Penelope smoothed her hair back and smiled. "It's going to be another hot one, isn't it?"

"You can say that again. The chief is already complaining about the fuel patrols are wasting by leaving the air conditioner in the cars running." He looked toward the front door. "You want me to close that for you on the way out?"

She shook her head. "No. Not yet." She took a deep breath. "It gets hot so seldom that I just want to enjoy it."

"It never gets this hot."

She smiled. "Exactly."

The radio handset hooked to his pocket gave off static. "Barnaby, you there?"

"Sorry, official business calls," he said, giving Penelope an apologetic look. He turned slightly away and pressed the button to talk. "Sheriff here. What is it?"

"You coming back with those muffins anytime soon?"

Penelope laughed. "Real important business."

After telling Dispatch that he'd return shortly, he turned back toward her. "Call you tonight at home?"

She immediately averted her gaze. "Sure."

If he hesitated, he didn't share the reason. He merely told her to have a nice day, and suggested she not leave the door open too long in case the old air conditioner she had was unable to cool the room, and then left.

She sighed, watching as he got into his patrol car parked outside and pulled away, giving her a small wave.

What in the hell was she going to do?

PALMER STOOD WATCHING the construction foreman drive off in the same direction as the previous truck, holding his breath briefly to keep from inhaling the dust he left in his wake. He hadn't known John Nelson well, but he was familiar with his family. Their fathers had worked at the mill together and sometimes the two families would have barbeques with other mill workers' families. He'd been happy to award him the foreman contract when a line fifty men deep had appeared outside the trailer door that first day. And they'd both put their heads together to put the rest of the forty-nine to work by month's end.

So what in the hell had happened?

He stared at an unfamiliar car that had been parked on the other side of Nelson's truck, blocking it from view until now. An upscale, late model that few in the small, blue-collar town would be able to afford.

Palmer turned toward the trailer and pulled open

the door, not stopped until he stood staring at the man taking complete liberty behind his desk inside.

None other than Manolis Philippidis himself.

"No work here," the older Greek said without looking up.

Palmer grimaced and rubbed his chin. "That's funny, because I thought I was the one hired to say that."

Manolis looked up. "Palmer!" He rose to his feet and edged around the desk to give him one of those half-handshake, half-hug deals that Palmer found annoyingly noncommittal. Go one way or the other, was his take.

"What brings you to Earnest?" he asked, stepping back.

Manolis waved a hand around. "Just wanted to see how things were going."

On the scale of Philippidis holdings, Palmer's present initiative had to rate somewhere between the least and nonexistent. Certainly nothing to attract the hands-on participation of the man himself. Christ, he'd handled business deals a hundred times the value of this endeavor and not only had Manolis not participated, he'd barely acknowledged the final result.

So what was he doing here now?

More importantly, why was he firing his personnel?

Palmer cleared his throat. "I just ran into John Nelson outside."

Manolis nodded, but didn't offer anything.

"He says you let him and the others go?"

"Yes. Yes, I did." Manolis stared into his face, as if

trying to ferret out how he felt about the move. Palmer didn't give off vibes one way or the other. His only intention was to find out why.

"Are you shutting me down?" he asked.

"No. No, I'm not shutting you down." Manolis leaned to the side and picked up a sheath of papers. "I just brought you a list of people I'd like you to work with."

Palmer raised his brows as he accepted the list. "I wasn't aware you had contacts in Earnest."

"I don't." Manolis grinned. "Outside of you, that is."

"And these men?"

"They'll be coming in from other sites."

Outsiders.

Palmer tried to hide his grimace, but must have failed because Manolis asked, "Do you have a problem with that?"

"Problem? No. I don't have a problem." He put the papers back down on the desk. "But I thought part of the bargain that we struck is that I would have complete autonomy in getting this thing off the ground."

Manolis began to walk toward the door, putting his arm across Palmer's shoulders so that he was forced to walk with him. "You do. You're running things. Nothing changes that."

"Except when it comes to personnel."

Manolis shrugged. "I have other men who have been with my companies a long time who need work."

Somehow Palmer doubted that.

He followed the wealthy Greek outside.

"When can I expect to see them?" he asked.

"Today. Tomorrow. The next day."

"And you? How long are you in town?"

"Pardon?"

"How long do you plan to stay?"

"Oh, I'm not staying."

He'd just driven down from Seattle to fire Palmer's employees.

Nothing about the past five minutes sat well with Palmer. And he had the sinking sensation that nothing in the immediate future was going to sit well with him either.

"Is there any place in town to have a good meal?" Manolis asked. "I haven't had breakfast yet."

Palmer told him of the diner, but curiously left out Penelope's place, which he knew served muffins and coffee.

"Good. I'll be going then. Unless you'd like to join me?"

Palmer grinned, the invitation clearly more rhetorical than genuine. "No, thank you. You go ahead." He looked back at the trailer. "I'm going to have to make a few phone calls—you know, to let people know that they no longer have the jobs I gave them."

Manolis's quiet chuckle as he walked toward his car set Palmer's back teeth on edge.

6

OKAY, THIS WAS RIDICULOUS. Every car that passed, every time the door opened, Penelope found herself hoping it would be Palmer. She hadn't felt this full of restless anticipation since...well, since the last time he'd played a role in her life.

She sat at her computer in the back of the shop, emailing order confirmations and printing packing slips and labels, checking stock. While locally her sales had taken a sharp nosedive, her online business was flourishing. Seemed ironic, somehow. But at least she was able to keep the front doors open when so many others had to close.

The sun reflected off a moving object. She leaned far back in her computer chair for a better glimpse of the street outside, and nearly fell over. She grabbed the edge of the desk with her hands and planted her feet to balance herself.

This was getting farcical. She wasn't a teenager given

over to flights of fancy. And while things had gotten hot and heavy last night, there was no reason it had to progress any further than it already had. She'd been down that route with Palmer once already. And knew all too well the dead end that awaited her.

You should have told him...

The words echoed in her mind, rendering her still for a long moment.

There had been little time for words last night. He'd shown up at her back gate, unfairly tempted her with memories in the gazebo. There had been no room for rational thought, much less conversation of any import.

And now?

Okay. So now that she both literally and figuratively had her feet back under her, she needed to think this thing out. She had to tell him. What remained was when and where.

The when was easy. As soon as possible. The where...

Her thighs grew damp. It would have to be somewhere neutral. Someplace where he couldn't lean forward and crowd out her thoughts with emotion. A public place.

She glanced out the front windows again, but this time for legitimate reasons. The diner...no, too many ears and well-tuned antenna. Her gaze settled on a good choice. The pub. At lunch the place would be only half full. She could get a booth away from the others, put money in the jukebox so music would drown out anything else...

And she would tell him.

Penelope rubbed her palms against the lap of her dress several times.

Now, she had to implement her plan…

PALMER PACED BACK AND FORTH in the narrow trailer, tightly holding his cell to his ear. Well over an hour had passed since Manolis Philippidis had driven off down the gravel road, leaving him wondering just what in the hell was going on.

"Christ," he said to his old friend and sometime business associate Caleb Payne. "I should have seen this coming. But, damn it, I didn't."

Caleb chuckled in his ear. "If I'd known what you two were up to, I could have warned you."

But he hadn't known. Because Manolis had asked Palmer not to tell him. Apparently for very good reason.

"If I were you, I'd pull up stakes now and head back for the east coast," Caleb told him. "Before it's too late."

"Too late for what?"

"Too late for you to get out from under Philippidis's black thumb."

Palmer stopped pacing and ran his free hand through his hair several times. The option wasn't one for him. It had taken him nearly fifteen years to come home. He wasn't going to turn tail and run straight back out. Not knowing how his father was currently living—or barely living. Not after making promises it appeared he couldn't keep.

Not after having tasted Penelope's sweet mouth again.

"Palmer?" Caleb said. "You still there?"

"Yeah. And I'm going to stay here."

Silence.

A beep indicated he had another call coming in. He looked at the cell's display screen, surprised to see "Penelope's Possessions" there.

"Thanks, Caleb. Can I call you back?"

"Only if you plan on taking me up on my advice. Or for a pickup game of b-ball."

He gave a wry smile and said goodbye, in a rush to take the other call.

"Penelope?"

No response.

Damn. She must have been switched over to voicemail.

He began to take the phone from his ear to check it when he heard someone speak.

"Penelope?" he said again.

"Yes. Yes, it's me. Sorry. I guess I'll never get used to someone knowing it's me before I've said hello."

Palmer edged around his desk and sat down in the chair, enjoying the sound of her voice in his ear.

"I'm the one who should be apologizing. I should probably allow the caller to identify themselves before calling them by name."

"But then it wouldn't be efficient. And if it's one thing you always were, it was efficient."

He didn't know if that was an insult or a compliment. "In the scheme of things, I think I'd prefer to be called unforgettable."

"Oh, you're very definitely unforgettable, Palmer."

Was that a wistful tone in her soft voice?

She cleared her throat. "Look, I'm calling because I want to see you."

Palmer's grin was full.

"Wait. That didn't come out right," she said. "What I meant to say is that we need to talk."

"I think I preferred it the other way."

"Yes, well, that's why I reworded it."

"Because you don't want to see me."

She sighed in obvious exasperation. "Can you please be serious for just a moment?"

Normally, he didn't have a problem with that. He was usually all business all the time. But with her, he couldn't help himself.

"Serious," he repeated. "Right. So, go ahead."

It took her a moment to respond as he leaned back in his chair, wondering how she had the power to make him forget everything that had gone on that morning with a mere word from her mouth.

"Will you meet me at O'Brien's Pub? At two-thirty?"

"Late lunch?"

"I work while others take theirs, you know, in case they want to squeeze in some shopping."

"Ah. So it is lunch, then."

"It's a chance to talk."

"In public."

"Yes."

"Today?"

"Would be nice."

"Fine. Two-thirty at O'Brien's then."

"Good."

"Shall I bring anything?"

"To a pub?"

"You're right."

"Goodbye, Palmer."

"Goodbye, Penelope."

"ASK AND YOU SHALL RECEIVE."

Penelope looked up to see her grandmother come inside the shop, holding a box.

She forced her body to relax, surprised she was so tense following her conversation with Palmer. "Thanks, Gran."

Agatha put the box of muffins down on the counter. "I didn't realize that it was such an emergency."

"What is?"

"Muffins."

She took the box and began filling the glass case with them. "Not an emergency. But since this is one of the bestselling items, it's good to have them on hand."

"What happened to the first batch?"

Her movements slowed.

"Sold out," she said without further explanation.

"Ah. That nice Sheriff Barnaby took them back to the office again, didn't he?"

Penelope let the empty box drop to her side. "Why did you bother asking again?"

Agatha shrugged. "In case there existed one chance in five thousand that your answer would be different."

"Maybe next time."

Agatha sighed and leaned against the case. "Maybe never."

If only she knew.

"What was that?"

Penelope squinted at her. "What?"

"I could have sworn you just said something."

Great, now she was speaking aloud her most repressed thoughts. Not a good idea. "I didn't say anything. Maybe it was the CD."

She had New Age music piped in over the shop's sound system.

"Not likely," her grandmother said. She eyed the fresh muffins and then shocked Penelope by cupping her breasts over her cotton top. "While I was watching those puppies rise back at the house, I was thinking that maybe it's long past time I do a little rising of my own."

Penelope choked.

"What do you think? Should I go up one or two cup sizes?"

She gaped at Agatha. "You can't possibly be serious?"

"Why can't I be?"

She made a face as her grandmother continued her breast exam. "Gram, you're seventy years old."

"And your point is?" She finally released her breasts, but still considered them. "Women my age are having plastic surgery all the time."

"Do you have any idea how much it costs to do that?"

She shrugged. "So I'll just have my sugar daddy pay for the surgery for me."

"Sugar..." Penelope held up her hands. "On second thought, no. I don't want to know." She moved down the counter. "Now if you'll excuse me, I have work to do."

Her grandmother looked around. "Yes, I can see that. They're just knocking down the door."

"The internet, Nana. The internet."

"Sure. Okay." She twisted her lips. "A body knows when it's no longer welcome somewhere."

If that were the case, then she would have left five minutes ago.

"I'll just go over to the diner and see what new gossip is circulating." She waggled her brows. "Who knows? It might just have to do with you."

7

OKAY, ON A SCALE FROM one to ten, this idea perhaps didn't rate the high nine that Penelope had hoped.

She sat in a back booth at O'Brien's Pub, trying to ignore the way everyone watched her. It was a day not unlike every other day in her life, but for reasons she would prefer not to pursue, the buzz of gossip seemed to be following her around town.

So she didn't go to the pub often. It didn't mean she didn't come here at all. She took an occasional meal here, as did everyone else in town at one time or another.

But now that Palmer was in town…

She realized what the gossips would make of her choosing a remote booth in the darkest part of the pub and hit her knees on the table as she got up quickly. She limped to a table more in the middle and sat down, smiling at the waitress who watched her curiously. "I think I like this one better."

Great. Just great. If they weren't gossiping about

her already, they would be now. Although, she'd rather they discuss her musical-booths bit over any speculation about her and Palmer.

She moved her glass of soda around on the damp napkin and looked at her watch. She'd gotten there ten minutes early. Which meant that he should be getting here—

"Hi."

She looked up to find him standing next to the table.

If the place had been buzzing before, now it was downright quiet.

The lunch crowd had pretty much moved on, leaving the small handful of regulars that lingered at the bar, a couple of men at a front booth, and the waitress and bartender. None of them made any secret of their interest in her and Palmer.

"May I?" he asked, gesturing toward the empty seat across from her.

"Sure, yes, yes. Sit."

She forced a swallow of soda down her tight throat. Let them talk. A little town gossip was better than being somewhere alone with Palmer where he could easily exploit her raw feelings for him.

The problem was, his sitting opposite her made everyone else fade quickly into the background...and the public setting didn't make her any less aware of him or her knee-melting reaction to him.

"So..." he said, giving her that half-grin that set the

butterflies in her stomach to fluttering. And when paired with his own expression of surprise, as if he'd just realized something, they might as well have been alone in the gazebo, because Penelope knew that if he leaned across the table to kiss her, she'd kiss him back. And more.

She broke eye contact. He wouldn't lean across that table. Not here. Which is exactly the reason why she'd chosen the meeting place.

Now if only she could remember why.

"Thanks, um, for coming," she said.

He waved for the waitress. "Have you eaten yet?" he asked.

"Huh? Oh. No."

He placed an order for two house specials. Penelope didn't bother to ask what it was. No matter what was put in front of her, she wouldn't be able to touch a bite of it. Not considering what she had to tell him. That sat like a boulder in the middle of her throat.

"I'm glad you called," he said.

She squinted at him.

"I'm getting the feeling that I'm not going to feel the same way by the end of the conversation."

She tried for a smile, but failed. What she had to tell him would set his world on its ear.

Which made it doubly obvious that she had picked the exact wrong place.

How could she possibly dump what she had to say in his lap in a pub? Within the earshot of what would amount to the entire town by the time the handful of patrons gained access to a phone?

"I don't know if this was such a good idea," she whispered to herself.

He leaned forward and touched her hands where they cupped her glass of soda. "Any reason for me to get to see you is a good reason, Penelope."

She searched his face. "Is it? I'm not so sure you're going to think that way later."

"Why don't you let me be the judge of that?"

She slid her hands out from under his, incapable of clear thought when he was touching her.

"Look, Penelope, I want to apologize for last night…"

Was it really less than twenty-four hours ago that she'd practically crawled onto his lap in the gazebo? Wanted him so badly she'd thought she'd spontaneously combust if she couldn't feel him?

Impossible. Incredible.

She cleared her throat. "That's okay."

He chuckled and sat back. "That was convincing."

"Sorry. It's just that…"

It was just that once she had a chance to say what she had to…well, he wouldn't have that friendly look on his face.

"I don't think it's a good idea for, um, us to see each other…" she began.

"Because of the sheriff?"

"What? Oh. You mean Barnaby." Her frown deepened.

She'd forgotten about him. Not good. What did that say about their situation? Nothing that she hadn't already known, really. But it didn't make things any easier.

"No…I mean, yes," she said.

Penelope took a deep breath and then released it, her shoulders finally relaxing. "Is it your mission in life to make things difficult for me?"

His grin widened.

"Thought so. Well, then. You'll be very happy to hear that you're succeeding admirably."

The waitress brought their meals. And much to her chagrin and amusement, the beer-battered fish and chips looked very appetizing.

Accepting that she had picked the wrong place to break such serious news, and understanding that it had waited fifteen years and wouldn't change if she shared it today, tomorrow or next week, she rethought her plan.

If she also was more than reluctant to change the way he was looking at her now—as if the sun rose and set on her and he'd like nothing more than to lean across the table—she wasn't owning up to it.

"So," she said, "what sort of work brings you back to Earnest?"

It struck her as odd that she hadn't asked him the question last night. She supposed the reason was that she already had secondhand knowledge of his plans. He was working with some Greek tycoon who had a grudge against the Metaxas family to bring some sort of green company to town.

Still, from his expression, that didn't tell the whole story.

And she had the feeling that she wasn't going to get it, either. At least not during this public lunch.

But his frown did tell her one thing—he wasn't happy with the way things were currently going.

"I'm overseeing the start-up of a company I hope will replace some of the jobs lost."

"Overseeing? So you don't...own it?"

His chewing slowed. "No, I don't own it. But I wish I did. I hit a road bump this morning that slowed me down considerably."

"Oh?"

He shook his head as he wiped his mouth with a napkin. "It's not something I can share right now. I'm still trying to wrap my head around the development."

"Nothing too serious, I hope?"

He fell silent, looking into her face for a long moment. Finally, he smiled again. "Not anymore."

The front door opened and closed again. Penelope looked over to find that the older of the two Metaxas brothers, Troy, had just come in. He looked in her direction and she waved, but he must not have seen it. Instead, he walked to the bar.

Why did she have the feeling that someone had called him to let him know that Palmer was there?

Word had it that the Metaxas brothers were very interesting in having a sit-down with Palmer. When she'd heard the rumor, she'd wondered why they didn't just go to the trailer on the outskirts of town where everyone knew Palmer had set up shop. It wasn't like he was an unreasonable man.

Now, she got the distinct impression that Troy Metaxas had done essentially what she had: waited until he could meet Palmer in a public place.

PENELOPE LOOKED MUCH BETTER than she had when he'd sat down at the booth. The knowledge brought Palmer a measure of relief. She'd looked so pale, her face so pinched, he'd been half afraid of what she was going to say.

But now she conversed easily, and was eating, which had always provided him with a deep sense of satisfaction and fascination. All people had to eat. It was just the way that Penelope did so gave him a front row seat to a scene of wonder.

She'd told him once that she had to be the least sexy person alive. But he knew differently. It was there, her innate sexuality, everywhere. In the way she opened her full mouth to take in a French fry, stopping midway to cut it in two with her even, white teeth. In how her tongue darted out to slide along her bottom lip. The almost silent humming sounds she made, a deep murmur in her throat in approval of the food.

She had no idea that she was, and had always been, the sexiest person he'd known.

He suspected she thought otherwise because of her choice of clothes, typically loose-fitting with high necks.

What she didn't know was that the uninhibited way she swayed her hips when she walked…the slope of her shoulders and the tendency she had of tilting her head slightly as if tempting a kiss to the side of her neck… it drove him absolutely wild. And forget the way she absently rubbed her hand along her opposite arm when she was deep in thought, a long, slow caress that left him yearning to feel those fingertips touching certain areas of his anatomy.

In fact, he was finding it nearly impossible not to reach out right now and haul her over the table until she was sitting in his arms.

"So what is it you wanted to talk to me about?" he asked, despite his fear that he wasn't going to like what she had to say.

Where her attention had been solely on him since he'd arrived, now she gazed at someone else across the room. He glanced over, trying to place the dark-haired man who had just entered.

"Someone else with whom I've got to compete?"

She blinked at him. "What?"

He nodded in the direction she'd been looking. "Someone else you're dating, besides the sheriff?"

"Palmer, I…" She twisted her lips and pushed her half-eaten plate of food away. "This isn't some sort of competition."

"Isn't it?"

She merely stared at him.

"So I've won then?"

"What?" she asked again.

"If this isn't a competition, then it means I've won."

"I don't understand your view of the world." She took a deep breath, smiled, and then let it out. "I think I'm lacking a body part or two."

"As in a pair?"

Her short laugh stirred something low in his belly.

"You're the one who brought up the male anatomy."

"For the purpose of demonstrating a point."

He shrugged. "I'm doing the same."

"I meant nothing sexual."

He held her gaze for a long moment, refusing to give ground. "Didn't you? Let me get you alone for five seconds and I think I can prove differently."

She averted her gaze and a cloud seemed to eclipse her eyes. "Well, that's never been a problem, has it?"

He puzzled that one over. "I don't know. I'm beginning to think that maybe it is…"

She considered him with interest even as Palmer became aware that the man who had walked in was now heading in their direction.

He looked up just as the unwanted visitor drew even with their table, prepared to tell him the lady was busy. Only he didn't appear interested in Penelope. Rather, he was staring at him.

8

"YOU DON'T REMEMBER ME, do you?" the stranger asked.

Palmer frowned. "No, I'm sorry, I don't. Should I?"

Penelope put her napkin down on top of her plate. "Palmer, this is Troy Metaxas. You remember. You two played football together at Earnest High."

Metaxas.

Ah. Yes.

Palmer rubbed the back of his neck as he stood up to shake the other man's hand. "Troy. Yes, I remember now." He tried for a grin. "Nice to see you."

Troy smiled but didn't appear convinced. "I don't mean to interrupt, but I was hoping that once you were done with lunch perhaps you and I could talk."

Palmer raised his brows. "Here? Now?"

"If you don't mind."

He glanced at his watch, then at Penelope, and said, "Sure. I can spare a few minutes or so."

"Glad to hear it." Troy gestured toward the bar. "I'll be waiting over there for you. Take your time. I'm in no hurry."

Palmer got the exact opposite impression. And judging by the expressions on the other patrons' faces as they openly watched the exchange, they felt the same way.

"I'm sorry, Penelope," Troy said, looking more genuine. "I hope I didn't ruin your lunch."

"Actually, we were just finishing," she said.

Palmer quickly interjected, "I'll see you over there in a few, Troy."

He sat down, providing both a period on the statement, and refusing Penelope easy escape.

Troy took the hint and left them alone.

Penelope leaned forward. "Well, that was awkward."

"Why should it have been awkward?"

"Well, you know..."

"Because we're in competition with each other?" He grinned, bringing their conversation back full circle.

Penelope's mouth fell open. "Are you serious?"

"Couldn't be more."

She picked up her purse and took out money.

"I've got it," he insisted.

"Fine. Thank you." She closed her purse and began to shift from her seat.

Palmer reached out and grasped her hand. "But I'm

not letting you go until you tell me why you wanted to see me."

"It can wait."

"Why? Because Troy Metaxas wants to talk to me?"

"No." She looked surprised. "Because two minutes after you sat down I figured out this is absolutely the wrong place to say what I have to say."

He didn't like the sound of that. "So that means another meal, then?" he asked, trying to find something positive in her statement.

"No. It means another meeting. But I have to decide where. And when."

"Name them and I'm there."

If it were possible for someone to both relax and tense up, he suspected he'd felt it then, just under her skin.

She slowly removed her arm. "I'll call you."

"I'll be waiting."

PENELOPE WALKED QUICKLY from the pub, barely acknowledging the others with a smile. She stopped on the sidewalk outside in order to adjust to the hazy summer light, and to take a deep breath of the heavy, unfamiliar air.

In fact, everything she felt was so foreign to her that she might as well have been on another planet.

Where were the cooler temperatures she was used to in the Pacific Northwest? The refreshing breezes? The more moderate sunshine she didn't want to run away from, but rather bask in? Better yet, the rain?

And just where in the hell had she put her common sense? And how was she going to go about finding it?

She looked up and down the mostly empty street and then crossed, walking up the half a block to her shop, her step quick, her heartbeat even quicker.

Would there ever come a time when she didn't feel so utterly…intoxicated by Palmer DeVoe? Mesmerized? When she could have a conversation and not think about sex and having it with him every single moment they were together?

Would she ever be able to share with him the secret she'd kept between her and her grandmother and great-aunt for fifteen years?

A car horn honked and she jumped, not having seen anyone in the road.

"Sorry, Penny. I didn't mean to scare you," Barnaby said as he lowered the window in his squad car.

"That's okay. I'm not quite myself today." She swallowed hard and clutched her purse to her side even harder. "It must be the weather."

He appeared doubtful as he looked at her and then across the street at the closed pub door. "I think we'll all be glad when this…front moves on."

Why did she get the distinct impression that he wasn't talking about merely the heat wave? And that he'd known where she'd been and who she'd been with?

She curved her free hand around her neck and moved

her damp hair away from the back. Of course, he would know. Just as the others had called Troy Metaxas, they'd probably called Barnaby as well.

"Well, I'd better get back to the shop," she said.

"Call you later?"

"I'll talk to you then."

Suddenly, the weather wasn't the only thing that was stifling.

PALMER REMAINED AT the table for a long time after Penelope left. So far his homecoming wasn't turning out exactly as he'd hoped. Which reminded him of the reasons he'd left in the first place.

He frowned and got up from his seat, searching for where Troy was waiting for him. There. At the end of the bar. He headed in that direction, watching as the others who had gathered around Troy drifted away, leaving him alone by the time he approached.

Palmer slid onto a stool next to him.

"You want something to drink?" Troy asked.

"Yes. I'm getting the feeling I'm going to need it." He raised his hand and called for whatever was on tap. Neither of them said anything until pub owner Bobby Schwartz put an icy glass mug in front of him along with a bowl of mixed nuts and then moved back down the bar.

Palmer knocked back a couple of the peanuts and chewed before taking a long pull off the brew. "Why do I get the feeling this meeting isn't a coincidence?"

Troy gave him a wry smile that made him look more like the teen Palmer remembered. "Because you didn't get where you are by being stupid."

He chuckled.

He was aware of Troy's prior business deal with Philippidis, as well as how the plans fell apart when Troy's brother ran off with Manolis's much-younger fiancée. It was part of the reason he'd taken on the job himself. There was no way the Greek was going to work with the Metaxas brothers again, so why not forge ahead with the plans they'd begun? It would bring important jobs to the town and perhaps at some point the company he helped create might even end up with the Metaxases.

Best of both worlds, the way he saw it.

He asked Troy, "Is there anything in specific you wanted to talk to me about?"

"Are you going to make me take back the compliment I just threw your way?"

"Backhanded and all?" Palmer nodded. "Yes. Because, you see, I also didn't get where I am by doing the other guy's job for him."

"Point awarded."

"And taken."

Troy was standing rather than sitting and now propped his right foot on the brass rest. "How worried should I be?"

Palmer considered him for a long moment. "About what?"

"About your being in town."

He shrugged. "If you'd have asked me yesterday…I'd have said 'very.'"

"And today?"

Palmer frowned into his beer before taking another sip. "Get back to me tomorrow on that one."

"I'd heard your foreman was fired."

He snorted. "Not by me."

"I know."

Palmer put his glass down and turned a little more fully in his direction. "Well then it begs the question why you requested this impromptu meeting with me."

"I told you, I want to know how much of a threat you are."

"To…"

"To the plans my brother and I have for a company so similar to the one you're opening as to be hostile."

Palmer frowned. "Look…I don't know everything that went down between you, your brother and Philippidis, Troy—"

"Maybe you should."

"No. Maybe I shouldn't. I'm not here for personal reasons. I'm here for professional ones."

"I'm sure Penelope would like to hear that."

Palmer winced.

"Philippidis has no intention of helping this town," Troy said. "I don't know how he plans on using you, but trust me, that's exactly what he's doing. And the end result is not going to be pretty."

"Why don't you let me worry about that?"

Troy narrowed his gaze. "If it were only my ego on the line, I would. I'd gladly go head-to-head with you, let the best man win."

"But…"

"But this isn't about you and me. And this isn't a harmless scrimmage or pickup game of tackle football."

"Well, then, Troy, why don't you tell me what it's about?"

"Revenge, pure and simple. Philippidis won't stop until he sees me and my family bankrupt—"

"I thought this wasn't about your ego."

Troy held up a hand, a tight smile revealing how much of his ego was involved. "Let me finish. He won't stop until he bankrupts not only my family, but anyone even remotely associated with us. Including this town and everyone in it."

Palmer eyed him for a long moment. He'd always known Troy to be an upstanding sort of guy, not given to exaggeration or underhanded moves. Unlike the man Palmer worked for, no matter how much he argued differently.

Of course, fifteen years had a way of changing a man.

"Is that it?" Palmer asked.

"What?"

"I asked if that was it. Your wanting to know whether or not I am a threat?"

Troy took his foot off the rest and stood straight. "That's it."

Palmer pulled out a bill from his back pocket that would cover their drinks and his lunch with Penelope and waved it at the owner before putting it on the bar. He stood up next to Troy and held out his hand. The other man took it with a measure of wariness.

"Then my answer is yes. I am a threat. And I'll go farther than that to say this is a competition. And while I usually subscribe to the 'all's fair in love and business' line of thought, I'll promise to keep it fair if you will."

Troy looked doubtful. "I can't talk you out of it? Perhaps offer to bring you on board with us?"

"Now, that's not playing fair now, is it?" He grinned. "Good luck to you. May the best man win."

"So long as Earnest wins as well, I'm all for it," Troy said as he walked toward the door.

9

PENELOPE FELT LIKE A thousand tiny ants were running just under her skin, making it impossible to sit still, impossible to concentrate, and impossible to be around anyone else. So after an especially animated dinner with her grandmother and aunt—during which the two unconventional women had brainstormed new ideas on how they might go about getting her laid—she'd mumbled about having forgotten to do something at the shop and slipped out of the house.

Now, an hour later, with the town quiet but for a few people at the pub, she hefted another supply box from the storage room and plopped it down on the front counter, then opened the top to peer inside. Despite the heat, she hadn't turned on the air conditioner but instead had a fan running, the front and the back doors propped open to catch whatever breeze might blow outside. A thin sheen of sweat coated her skin, adding to her sense of quiet restlessness.

It wasn't fair.

Throughout the past hour, fragmented thoughts had emerged in her mind, taunting her, challenging her.

She ignored the latest as she had the previous ones, instead counting napkins as she took them out and stored them under the counter, following those with coffee cups and lids.

She'd spent much of the time so far filling electronic orders for shipping, a pile of which sat by the front door waiting for the postman tomorrow. She'd accomplished more that night than during the entire day. Of course, now she didn't have customers and friends coming in and out…or a late lunch with Palmer to deal with.

She finished unpacking the box and listlessly leaned against the top.

It wasn't fair, her mind repeated.

"You can say that again," she agreed.

It wasn't fair that he should look so good when most other men his age had gained weight and lost hair. It wasn't fair that he exuded a confidence befitting a much younger man.

It wasn't fair that he should make her want him even more now than she had back then.

Talk about being fair. She was blaming him for her physical condition when aside from a brief touch or two, he'd been the perfect gentleman at the pub.

Last night…

Well, last night had taken place in the shadows of the gazebo when both their guards had been down. When darkness had buffeted them from the rest of the world and amplified emotions that hadn't been stirred in much too long.

She pulled the box off the counter and used the cutters to collapse it, stashing it with others against the wall. Maybe Agatha and Irene were right. She needed to get laid.

Or, rather, it was long past time that she had an adult relationship in her life that didn't include her nosy roommates. That satisfied her needs all around, not merely in the bedroom.

It didn't help to know there were reasons why she hadn't had one. Reasons that well beyond pining over a lost high school sweetheart. But that didn't change the fact that here she was, a thirty-three year old woman, crushing on a man who had long since moved on.

She looked at the watch on her wrist and sighed, wondering what else she could do to push herself to the point of total exhaustion. To a spot where Palmer's grin didn't intrude on her thoughts every five seconds. When the hunger making it impossible for her to sit still for long periods would stop its incessant growling and allow her to entertain the notion of sleep.

Her feet carried her to the back room yet again...

PALMER HADN'T REALIZED how far or for how long he'd been walking until his feet began to protest...and he found himself standing outside Penelope's shop.

The front door was propped open, which struck him

as unsafe until he realized where he was. While Earnest was not without crime, any lawbreakers inevitably made The World's Dumbest Criminals list because someone always knew who they were, no matter how well they disguised themselves.

It was like that in a small town. And fell solidly into the plus category.

Unfortunately, so far he seemed to be endlessly discovering all the entries in the minus category.

After his lunch with Penelope, and his tense conversation with Troy Metaxas, he'd returned to the site to field phone calls from the various suppliers with whom he'd contracted. It appeared Manolis Philippidis had been very busy indeed during his time in the trailer this morning.

He'd finally left at sometime after five to return to a cold dinner at the B and B—no one was around and the covered tray had been left at his door with a note attached—and a night yawning emptily before him.

So he'd gone for a walk.

And walked and walked and walked. From the grounds of Earnest High on the east side of town, to the old creek to the west. To the front of his father's house where he'd stood just after sunset watching through the open curtains as the switching colors of the TV flashed across the face of a man he no longer knew.

He absently rubbed his chin. What was he talking about? He'd never known his father.

He'd moved on from there, exchanging hellos with

a few of the more friendly residents, and withstanding open stares from the rest. He'd half expected to find the sheriff's car dogging his steps at some point, and found himself welcoming the idea, if only because it would give him an excuse to focus his thoughts outside rather than within.

And now he stood in front of Penelope's shop, longing to go in, yet not daring to.

When he'd originally received her call earlier in the day, he'd expected she would tell him at lunch to keep his distance. Public places were always the perfect venues for such conversations. But since she hadn't told him to lay off, and had indicated that perhaps the pub wasn't the best place to speak her piece, he wondered what it was, exactly, that she had to say.

Movement caught his eye from inside the shop. He watched as Penelope came out of the back room carrying a box, stepping purposefully in his direction. He thought she'd spotted him and was going to give him what for for standing outside her place like some sort of stalker.

Instead, she placed the box on a pile of others near the door, presumably ignorant to his presence.

Damn, but she looked good. Small tendrils had escaped the rubber band that held her long hair at the nape of her neck and lay against her beautiful face, damp and curly.

His gaze dropped to the V of her dress, finding her skin there shiny. He took in the fact that she had the fan running, waging a losing battle against the still warm temperatures. The back of his shirt was also damp from his walk. He'd been so lost in thought, he hadn't even registered the heat. But now he was overly aware of it… along with a heat of an entirely different variety.

Penelope stretched her neck and then went still, as if sensing she wasn't alone. She stepped to the door and looked to the left and then the right, her gaze colliding with his.

"Palmer," she said on a rush of air.

He took his hands out of his pockets and held them palm up. "I was walking by the place and…"

The words sounded unconvincing to his own ears, so he stopped.

She leaned against the doorframe and crossed her arms under her breasts, bringing them into relief under her loose-fitting dress. Palmer couldn't help himself as he took in the plumped-up flesh.

"The thought of sitting at the B and B alone…" he offered.

She sighed. "Tell me about it. I couldn't stay home with those two busybodies."

He grinned. "How is your grandmother?"

She shrugged lightly. "The same."

"Meaning…"

"She's crazy as ever."

He chuckled, remembering several run-ins with the older woman in times gone by. There was one time when she'd caught him in Penelope's bedroom and chased him out with a broom, running all the way down the block—and half of the next—after him.

He voiced the thought aloud and Penelope laughed.

"Yes, well, now she'd be doing the opposite."

"I don't understand."

"She'd be chasing you into my bedroom with the broom and then would use it to lock you inside."

His brows rose. "Really?"

She nodded.

"So she's not the same. She's crazier than she was back then."

Her smile was brighter than the scattering of lights inside the shop.

"So what are we doing here, then?" he asked.

"Pardon me?"

"I'm just saying that I'd enjoy being on the other side of your grandmother's broom so long as it meant spending uninterrupted time with you."

She looked down, her face serious instead of smiling. Not his intention.

Then she looked up. "No one's interrupting now..."

THE CORNER OF A BOX jabbed into Penelope's shoulder blade, and she nearly tripped over a plastic bottle of glass cleaner as Palmer advanced on her in the cramped confines of the shop's back room.

Finally, she found an accommodating spot against an old metal table, her breath rushing from her body as he threaded his fingers through her hair, shaking it out from the loose twist she'd put it in earlier.

Then he pressed his mouth against hers and it wouldn't have mattered if she'd been standing on hot coals, or lying on a bed of nails so long as he was kissing her.

She watched his half-lidded eyes as he tilted his head one way, then the other, taking his time as he reacquainted himself with her lips. She pressed her palms against the expanse of his chest, not to push him away, but to make sure he was really there.

She was very pleased to find he was.

Last night he'd caught her off guard. And while she hadn't expected to find him outside the shop tonight, she was more prepared emotionally...and receptive to the need that suffused her body at the mere sight of him.

It had been so long. So very, very long since she'd given herself permission to feel a physical connection to another person. While she might have kissed a date, or participated in a bit of tickle and grab, she'd never been one hundred percent present. There had always been something there between her and the other person. Something that prevented her from completely shutting off her mind and giving herself over to the world of pure sensation.

Now...

Well, now as Palmer gently cupped her right breast through her dress, her knees nearly gave out from under her, her response was so great.

She broke off the kiss and restlessly licked her lips before leaning into him again, winding her arms around his body and pulling his hips flush to hers. She was instantly aware of his own arousal as it pressed against her lower belly.

He groaned, a guttural sound that never quite made it from his mouth as his hands went from her hair to her breasts to her hips as if he didn't know where to touch her first. He checked for a catch on her bra in the front and then the back and then gave up, returning to caressing her through the fabric, bringing her nipples to stiff, aching peaks.

She tugged on his shirt, freeing it from his pants and pushing it up and over his head rather than unbuttoning the front. She kissed her way down his jaw to his collarbone, her fingers running along his bare chest and abdomen. His skin was hot and smooth, his muscles impossibly toned.

Her knuckles brushed against his stomach as she slid her fingertips inside the front of his pants. His quick intake of breath caused a shiver to travel down her spine and back up again as she clumsily fumbled with his belt.

He chuckled softly. "You'd think we'd have gotten better at this…"

He helped her with his pants and she helped him with her sport bra that had no catch for him to pop.

Finally, they were both naked under the dim, overhead light, their breathing ragged, their bodies on fire as they stared at each other. In Palmer's eyes, she saw the shadows of years past. In her heart, she felt them.

He leaned in to kiss her and she surrendered fully. Not just to him. But to her own need.

10

PALMER WAS HAVING A hard time dragging a deep enough breath into his lungs. It was more than the muggy night. Just looking at Penelope, completely stripped of her clothes, and of her defenses, did him in.

Standing before him as she was, her hair a dark tangle around her beautiful face, her belly rounded, her womanhood in shadow, the past meshed so intrinsically with the present that it knocked him back on his heels. She'd been his first. And still held him more in awe than any other woman he'd met.

He ran his fingertips over her jaw and pressed the pad of his thumb against her plump bottom lip. No lipstick. No gloss. Just one hundred percent Penelope.

She opened her mouth and took his thumb inside, lightly nipping before closing her lips around the digit and sucking.

Palmer groaned, his reaction as complete as if she'd

been focusing that attention on another area of his anatomy.

He kissed her hard, filled with a burning need to bury himself inside her. To be surrounded by her. She curved her bare foot around his calf and he smoothed his hand down her hip to her thigh, lifting her to the table. The metal top was cool. He pushed aside a couple of boxes to make room and then gripped her knees, parting them slowly.

Penelope's head fell back as she braced herself against her arms and thrust her hips slightly forward, allowing him full access.

Sweet Jesus, but she was beautiful.

There was no waxing for her, just a neat trim that perfectly accentuated her silken folds. He was surprised to see his hands trembling slightly as he slid them up from her knees until his thumbs joined between her thighs. He tunneled them into her springy curls until they hit the velvety flesh beneath. She gasped and her hips bucked involuntarily even as he explored the uneven length of her swollen folds before parting them, opening the glistening flesh to his hungry gaze.

Penelope curved her feet around his hips, pulling him closer.

"Please," she whispered restlessly before kissing him, her hands holding his head still.

It took no time—yet forever—for Palmer to get the condom out of the back pocket of his jeans on the floor and sheath himself. Then, finally, he was back right where he wanted to be, Penelope ready and wet and waiting for him.

He stared into her heavy-lidded eyes, his own breathing loud in his ears. Sweat trickled down his back and through the valley between her breasts. He bent down to lick the salty trail, his thumbs reclaiming their spot between her legs as he prepared her for him. Then he entered her in one long, soulful stroke...and froze.

Yes...

If the anticipation had been torture, the destination was blindingly brilliant.

Penelope's mouth stilled in an almost perfect O, and he swore he could feel the beating of her heart in the slick flesh that gripped him. He was afraid that if he breathed, if he moved, it would be all over before he'd even started.

He'd waited so very long for this moment. Not consciously. But being there now...he knew that she, that Penelope, was the one thing he'd missed most about Earnest. There was something...special about her. Something that inspired sensations that no other woman could come close to achieving. He could spend from now to the end of his days trying to figure out why.

But he'd much rather revel in feelings that grabbed and twisted and ground through his insides.

Leaving one of his thumbs resting against her stiff bud, he slid his other hand around her hips, drawing her nearer to the edge of the table. He flicked his thumb against her stiff tissue, taking triumph in the fact that she was as affected as he was when she instantly exploded around his pulsing erection.

Palmer ground his back teeth to hold off.

Not yet...not yet...

It took every lick of self-control he possessed not to empty his hot need into her. It would take very little to push him over the edge, even though he had every intention of enjoying the view for as long as humanly possible.

Oh, and what a lovely view it was, too. Penelope spilled over the top of the worktable, every inch of her glorious skin glistening, her nipples rigid peaks, her stomach expanding and contracting in time with her breathing. He leaned in and kissed her even as he withdrew and slid in to the hilt again, swallowing her gasp.

She lifted her knees, pressing them against his side and inviting him in deeper. He was only too happy to oblige as his thrusts increased in intensity, driving the mercury of his desire up and up and up further still. His heartbeat echoed in his ears and the emotions that had been churning through his body coalesced in his aching penis. He reached around her, cupping her supple bottom in his hands, lifting her slightly from the table as he pulled and pushed her in rhythm with his thrusts.

Then, finally, there was no more control to be had. It vanished in a bright flash of light. His movements ceased, his lungs froze, and his hips bucked. Apparently sensing his crisis, Penelope came again seconds after he did, the tightening of her slick muscles prolonging his orgasm. They clung together, their skin drenched, their bodies fixed.

Palmer distantly wondered how he'd gone so long without the magnificent woman in his arms...and how he could go about making sure he never went without her again....

PENELOPE WALKED the few blocks home. The town was quiet on normal nights, but she swore tonight she could hear the trees draw their sap closer and the dew settle onto the grass as she passed. Her entire body hummed and her heartbeat had yet to return to its regular rhythm.

Her memories were chock-full of making love to Palmer. But somehow her mind had dulled the vibrancy of their coming together.

That's why she hadn't had a serious relationship since then. Because she knew no one else would quite equal what she felt when she was with him. Only he knew exactly where to touch her. Only he knew how to slide his tongue against hers in just that way that made her hungry for more. Only he felt right nestled between her thighs as she held tight, never wanting to let him go.

The house was blessedly dark. She'd been afraid she'd have to face her grandmother and aunt and had purposely delayed her return home because of that. She couldn't seem to budge the grin from her face and feared it would be a dead giveaway to the twosome.

She let herself inside the unlocked front door, hung her purse on the coat tree and then took her shoes off one by one, so as not to make any more noise than she had to when she crept to her bedroom.

"No use tiptoeing. We know you're home. So you'd be better off coming in here and telling us what kept you so late."

Penelope briefly closed her eyes and drew in a deep breath. Damn.

She dropped her shoes to the floor near the door and walked toward the dark kitchen. Only the light from a flickering red candle in the middle of the table kept her from stubbing a toe against a chair leg.

"Here," her great-aunt said, pushing a chair toward her. "Sit down and pour yourself a glass of homemade sangria."

Her grandmother had her tarot cards out. Penelope twisted her lips.

"Who wants what answered?" Agatha asked.

Normally, the only time the tarot made an appearance was when one or the other of them had a question to which they didn't know the answer. Or a problem they couldn't see a way to solve.

"You're the one with the question," her aunt told her, pouring a sizable amount of sangria into a glass.

Penelope took it and downed a couple of swallows, fortifying herself for what was to come. "I have no questions."

Her grandmother looked at her from beneath lowered lids. "So you have it all figured out then?"

She forced herself to pause and not answer quickly. To do so would only be to encourage them. "As well as anybody," she said, purposely vague.

"Hunh," her aunt disagreed.

She started to get up. "While this is interesting and all, I'm beat..."

"Of course, you are. Considering that you've been out there having sex."

Penelope's gasp filled the room.

"Don't look at me like that, girl. I've been having it much longer than you have. I know what it looks like. What it smells like."

She smelled?

"Yup," Irene said, closing her eyes. "Musk...sweat...latex."

Penelope nearly knocked over her glass of sangria. "What?"

"You don't think we use condoms?" her grandmother asked. Then she waved her hand. "Oh, not for protection against pregnancy, although I understand if either of us really wanted to have a child or eight, and had enough money to pay a doctor, we could still do it." She made a face. "Do you realize that our age group is the one with the fastest growing new diagnoses of AIDS?"

Her great-aunt shook her head. "Seniors with AIDS. What is this world coming to? You suffer PMS and PMDD through your childbearing years. Sweat your way

past menopause thinking your reward is—finally!—
some sweet, exquisite unprotected sex. Then, bam!
Some skank starts spreading disease and you end up
stocking Trojans all over again."

"Skank?" Penelope leaned her forehand against her
hand. Just when she thought her grandmother and great-
aunt were incapable of surprising her, they pulled out a
doozy like this.

"Yes, skank. What would you call a woman going
around having sex willy-nilly?"

She stared at her. "Oh, I don't know? Grandma?"

Her aunt laughed. "I think she just called you a
skanky ho, Agatha."

Penelope's mouth fell open. Then she held up her
hands. "This conversation is beginning to have a decid-
edly Twilight Zone feel to it. I'm going to bed where I'm
assured that my dreams won't be half as disturbing."

"Or half as interesting," Irene said.

"Sit down."

Penelope blinked as she looked at her grandmother.
"What?"

"You heard me. Sit. I'm not finished with you yet."

"That's funny, because right now I'm more than finished with this conversation."

"That's because you don't want to tell us who you
had sex with."

"I haven't had sex!"

Both of them stared at her.

What, was it tattooed on her forehead? Some sort

of glowing letters like those on that ring in the hobbit movie that only appeared under intense heat?

She sighed and sat back down, fearful that they'd only follow her to her bedroom where there'd be no escape from the hell they were creating for her.

"Was it with that perfectly yummy Sheriff Barnaby?" her great-aunt asked. "What am I saying? Of course, it was. Who else is there?"

Her grandmother's gaze seemed to bore a hole right through her. "Who else, indeed?"

She glanced at the tarot cards she'd laid out before her and then tapped one. Penelope and her great-aunt leaned forward for a peek.

"The Hierophant!" her aunt said. Then she frowned. "But I thought the card for Barnaby was that mailman guy. The Page of Pentacles?"

"What else do you see?" her grandmother asked.

Penelope looked the standard full spread over. All the cards were in the major arcana. "Impossible," she whispered.

Never, in all the years since the two women had been reading tarot, had she seen only major arcana pop up.

"You rigged it," she accused.

"I did no such thing."

"So who's the Hierophant?" Irene wanted to know.

Both women looked at her.

She didn't appear to have a clue.

"I think we need to increase your blueberry intake," her grandmother said. "It's that Palmer DeVoe."

"Palmer DeVoe…but isn't he…?" Her aunt's eyes widened. "Oh, my."

"Mmm," her grandmother said, looking back down at the cards. "I see here that the two of them met earlier today…perhaps over a meal…"

"You do not." Penelope leaned forward.

"No, I don't. But I did hear about it."

Penelope sat back heavily in her chair and crossed her arms. "It's none of your business."

"Isn't it? Funny, but I think it's very much our business."

She got up from her chair, put her barely touched sangria glass in the sink and then stepped toward the hall. "That's my cue to leave."

"Have you told him yet, Penelope?"

If any words were capable of stopping her in her tracks, it was those.

11

PALMER READJUSTED HIS GRIP on the two reusable grocery bags he held and opened the front gate. The grass needed to be cut, the bushes were overgrown and the stench of what smelled like a dead animal assaulted his nose. He could only hope that it was a squirrel or another small animal that had perhaps gotten hit by a car and crawled into his father's yard to die instead of a forgotten pet.

Thankfully, the front door to the house was unlocked. Now he had but to hope that the same would apply to the screen door. It did.

Without knocking, he walked straight inside. "Pops? It's Palmer."

He hadn't known his father to own a gun, so he didn't believe he was in danger there. Although, as he'd seen firsthand, an awful lot could change in fifteen years.

"I brought you a few groceries. Thought you could use them." He walked through the living room. He'd been so fixated on the old man last night when he'd stood watching him through the front window that he hadn't take much note of anything else. Now, he noticed that everything in the room was as he remembered. Exactly as he remembered. Including the fake sprays of flowers his mother had liked to decorate the place with. Framed old school photos of him still dotted the walls, and needlepoint pillows still sat on the pale blue velvet sofa and chairs. What was different was that everything was faded and covered in years' worth of dust, as if the place had been deserted right after her death.

He cleared his throat of unexpected emotion and continued his monologue to let his father know he was there. "I'm just going to put the groceries in the kitchen…"

He drifted off as he came to a stop just outside the room in question. His father sat hunched over the narrow kitchen table that had been pushed up against the wall, dunking a jelly-topped cracker into a mug. He'd stopped eating at the sight of Palmer. Half the cracker fell into the mug and what looked like plain water splashed out.

"Good morning, Pops," he said, lifting the bags. "I brought you a few things I thought you might need."

Thomas snapped out of his momentary shock. He picked up the dish towel at his elbow and wiped his hands jerkily with it. "What in the hell are you doing here, boy?" He moved the mug out of the way along with a few crackers and a nearly empty jar of preserves. "I thought I made it clear that I wanted nothing to do with you."

The words didn't sting any less, but Palmer was prepared, unlike the first time around. Essentially, he'd decided to ignore the old man. Or at least any snide remarks he made. Lord knew he'd done it before. It shouldn't be too difficult to pick that skill back up again now.

He placed the bags on the chipped yellow linoleum counter and lifted the lids on the ceramic storage jars. The ones for coffee, sugar, tea and flour were all empty. And he doubted that any of the staples could be found in the small pantry or cupboards. He took the fresh supplies from the bags he'd brought and filled the jars and then opened the refrigerator. He picked up a quart of milk, sniffed the top and then dropped it into the nearby garbage bin, stocking fresh milk, eggs, butter and cheese inside before closing the door.

Turning, he placed a loaf of bread on the table in front of his father, then took his mug. As he suspected, water. He emptied the contents into the sink and then filled the teakettle and put it on a lit burner.

"Who do you think you are?" his father fairly sputtered, struggling to get to his feet. "No one asked you to bring this…stuff. No one invited you."

Palmer folded the bags.

"You don't belong here. You never belonged here."

He winced at the bitter words, but kept his council as

he placed a tea bag in the cup and waited for the water to boil.

"I'm talking to you, boy!"

His father grasped his arm. Palmer swung around to face him, staring squarely into an angry face he remembered all too well.

Thomas's DeVoe's milky-blue eyes bulged, but that's where the facial similarities ended. His father's unshaven jaw, the dark circles under his eyes, the unkempt, longish gray hair...they were all unfamiliar.

And if he wasn't mistaken, his father had shrunk a good five inches. Either that, or he only remembered him being taller.

Now the top of his head came to about Palmer's eyebrows.

"I heard you," he said evenly.

His father seemed to be registering the same changes in him. It hit Palmer like a fist to the gut to realize how he now resembled the man before him. He looked very much like his father at around the same age.

Thomas opened his mouth, presumably to say something else insulting. But instead of words, coughs wracked his thin body. He lifted a closed hand to his face and backed up until he could lean against the rickety table. Palmer reached out to steady him, but his father shook his hand off and then sat back down.

Palmer filled a glass with water and put it in front of him. The old man didn't touch it.

He turned back toward the counter and took a calming

breath. This was far more difficult than he would have imagined. His overwhelming desire was to make a bee-line for the door. But he didn't dare. For reasons he couldn't identify, it was important that he try to mend the crumbled bridges between him and his old man.

So he went about making tea and toast in silence and put both in front of his father on the table.

"Enjoy your breakfast," he said, gathering the bags and putting them under the sink where his mother had always kept them. "I'll be back for dinner."

"I don't want you anywhere near this place."

"Yes, well, I wanted a father who would be happy to see me. So it looks like neither one of us is getting what we want."

He left the house, trying to convince himself that he was doing this for the greater good.

"I'M SORRY I DIDN'T CALL LAST NIGHT," Barnaby sounded as apologetic as his words. "We had a three-car pile up over on Route 6 involving a fuel tanker. It was a mess."

Penelope bit her bottom lip and crossed the kitchen floor to the microwave where popcorn was popping, nearly getting knocked over by Thor in the process. It seemed odd somehow that Barnaby should be apologizing, considering what she'd been doing while he'd been busy seeing to an emergency.

Images of sweat-coated skin and soft gasps swept

through her mind and re-ignited the longing that seemed fused with her DNA.

She cleared her throat. "I hope everyone was okay."

"One of the victims had to be airlifted to Seattle, and oversight of the cleanup from the fuel spill took hours, but thankfully everything's back up and running this morning."

Penelope frowned at the dog running circles around her ankles. "Good. Good."

Tonight was reality show night with her grandmother and aunt. It's when they settled in front of the TV together, the snack food spread out on the coffee table in front of them. Penelope had just ducked into the kitchen to stick another bag of kettle popcorn into the microwave when the telephone had rung.

Now, Barnaby said, "You're not upset with me, you know, for not calling, are you?"

"Penelope!" her grandmother called. "David's about to find out about what Janice has been up to! Hurry it up already!"

She gave an eye roll as she said to Barnaby, "Upset? No, no. Of course not. Why would I be upset?"

"No reason. I guess. I just thought… Well, anyway. I just wanted to explain why I hadn't called."

"Thank you, Barnaby. I appreciate your thoughtfulness."

A trait that made it all the more difficult to live with herself after what happened between her and Palmer the night before.

But that wasn't the handsome sheriff's fault. She was on her own in the guilt department when it came to that.

"Penelope!" Her great-aunt this time.

"I'm on the phone!" she shouted.

"Ouch. I think you may have just broken my ear drum," Barnaby said.

"Sorry."

"That's all right." He paused for a moment, then added, "So…I was thinking that maybe we'd go out again this weekend?"

Penelope nearly swallowed her tongue as the dog now also barked at her. "What do you want?"

"Pardon me?"

She was destined for the flames of hell. "Not you, Barnaby. I was, um, talking to Thor."

"Oh. Good. That's a relief." He chuckled. "Sounds like a madhouse over there."

"You have no idea."

"What do you say? Should I pick you up Friday at eight?"

The dog overturned a pedestal holding a fern and she cursed. "Look, Barnaby, I've got to go. Why don't you try calling later in the week?"

"What? Okay. Sure."

"Good night."

"Good—"

She didn't wait for his response as she took the phone from her ear and pressed the disconnect button. "What is the matter with you?" she demanded of the insufferable canine. "You've eaten. You have water. You've been outside…"

He barked again as she righted the plant. Thankfully, it was one of her grandmother's fake ferns so there was no soil to clean up. While she worked magic in the garden, she had a tendency to kill whatever was inside the house.

"What? You want to go back outside?" She stood straight. "Fine. Let's go."

He fairly galloped to the door ahead of her, blocking her path as she tried to make her way around his furry butt. Finally, she leaned over him and opened the screen door. He hit it in his hurry to get outside, and she nearly fell onto the back porch.

"Oh, for God's sake," she muttered under her breath, regaining her balance and staring at her hand to make sure no major damage had been done.

The hair on the back of her neck stood on end.

Someone was there.

Thor hadn't needed to water the grass. He'd wanted to come out to greet his new old buddy.

Penelope slowly looked up.

Palmer.

He stood in the shadows near the gazebo, and she might not have made him out at all had Thor not run straight for him, planting his paws against Palmer's chest for a thorough ear scratch.

"Good boy," he said quietly, his words sending a thrill rushing over her skin.

Penelope looked behind her at the empty kitchen, wondering how long till the next commercial. After last night's impromptu tarot card reading, she was sure she didn't want her grandmother and great-aunt to discover Palmer in their backyard.

She quickly crossed the garden to meet him.

"I sent the dog telepathic messages to bring you out here," Palmer said with a grin. "I tried the same with you, but you appeared to be preoccupied."

It was all she could do not to say something along the lines of "I was on the phone with my boyfriend."

Instead, she whispered, "What are you doing here?"

The grin slid from his face. She was pretty sure she wasn't the cause of his sudden seriousness. Rather, she sensed that something had happened.

"What is it?" she asked.

"Can I talk to you?"

Penelope looked over her shoulder again. The clock was ticking until the show hit a commercial and her housemates came looking for her and the snack she had yet to return with.

"Please." Palmer's voice was low and somber.

Penelope eyed him in the dark. If she had been about to refuse him, any thought of doing so now was out of the question.

She grasped the back of Thor's collar. "Meet me around the corner in ten minutes," she said.

Palmer surprised her by leaning in to kiss her.

"Come on, boy," she rasped, tugging on the collar. "Let's get back inside."

12

PALMER LOOKED AT THE dashboard clock for the fifth time. It had been at least twenty minutes since he'd left Penelope in the garden. Had he gone around the wrong corner? Even though this had been the place he had waited for her so many times before, perhaps she had forgotten and meant the next block.

He rubbed the back of his neck. The tensions of the day had knotted up there, clinging to him like a bad scent. He wasn't sure why he'd sought Penelope out tonight. He'd figured that after what had happened at the shop, she might need some time to adjust.

A brief knock on the passenger window. Palmer leaned over and opened the door for her.

"Hi," she said, bending to look in at him.

"Get in," he invited.

She looked over her shoulder and then climbed inside.

And he knew immediately why he'd sought her out.

The knot in his neck began to ease merely having her sit next to him. The world suddenly seemed to make more sense. And although he hadn't realized he'd felt that way, he no longer felt so alone.

Alone.

Funny, that's the word that jumped out at him. For the past fifteen years he'd flown solo. But ever since returning to Earnest, he'd felt as if something was missing.

"Sorry I took so long…I can't believe I'm saying this, but I had to wait until the TV show was over and then faked a headache so I could lie down." She stared at him. "I actually snuck out of my bedroom window."

"You didn't?"

"I did." She laughed and then turned to stare out the window.

When he didn't say anything for a long moment, she asked, "What's wrong?"

Palmer grimaced as he started the car.

"Where are we going?" she wanted to know.

He gave a brief shrug. "I don't know. I think it might be better if we maybe drive around while we talk. You know, in case someone calls your boyfriend."

He'd meant it as a joke, but a glance at her pained face told him she didn't find it funny.

"Thanks for coming. I…" He turned left at the next corner. "I didn't know who else I could turn to."

And just like that he was telling her about his uneasy visits with his father over the past few days. About how he'd taken him groceries that morning, and the animosity he'd encountered. About how he'd arranged for a landscape company to go to his place and see to the lawn and how they'd reported back that his father had chased them off.

"You're kidding."

He shook his head. "No." He couldn't help a quiet laugh. "They say he turned the hose on them and wouldn't stop until they left."

She smiled.

"Have you seen that place? I mean, I almost didn't recognize it."

She nodded. "I've seen it. A couple of the neighborhood boys have mowed the lawn once or twice this summer, but the shrubs are overgrown and the flowers… well, I don't have to tell you."

"Yeah. I thought about doing it myself, but with everything that's going on with my business here…" He drifted off, not wanting to fill her ear with all that was happening. He could barely shoulder it all.

He cleared his throat.

"Anyway, I'd promised the old goat that I'd be coming back tonight to fix dinner…"

He turned onto the main highway that ran west out of town.

"You cook?"

"Huh?" He looked at her and then offered up a slow grin. "I do."

"Oh, I see. You grill."

"No, I cook. In fact, I make the best damn seafood linguine this side of the Pacific."

She smiled doubtfully.

"Okay, maybe in Earnest. But it's damn good, if I do say so myself."

"So did you go? To your dad's?" she asked.

He nodded. "Or, rather, I should say that I tried to. He wouldn't let me in." He tightened his hands on the steering wheel.

She didn't say anything. Merely sat waiting for him to continue.

"Funny, we never used to lock our doors. And this morning they were both open. Then I go back tonight and the screen door is locked tight and the inner door is closed." He dragged in a deep breath. "I waited, looked in the windows, but I couldn't see if he was home or not."

He explained how he'd put the groceries he'd bought down on the steps and went around the house, finding the source of the rotting smell he'd noticed in the morning by way of a dead squirrel. The back door was shut as well, with no lights on inside.

"Maybe he was out."

He gave her a long look.

She shrugged. "I hear that he goes to church every now and again. Maybe he made the nighttime service or something."

"I've never known my father to go to church."

"Well, perhaps it's time to accept that maybe you don't know your father very well."

She had a point there.

"What else do you know?" he asked.

It felt odd to be asking someone else about his own parent, but not as strange as he might have thought. At least not when it was Penelope.

"I know that he hasn't worked since the mill closed two years ago," she said. "Not unlike a lot of the men who worked there their entire lives."

He nodded, having gleaned at least that much from his father during his sporadic phone calls over the years.

"Has he…dated?" he asked.

Penelope's eyes widened. "What? I don't know. How should I know that?"

"The town is small—"

"It's not that small. Besides, I have my hands full trying to keep up with my grandmother and aunt…"

She fell silent.

"What?"

She stared through the windshield at their surroundings. "First I sneak out the window and now…" She squinted at him. "You aren't taking me to Makeout Cove, are you?"

Palmer raised his brows. He hadn't realized that's where he was heading, but it did indeed appear that he had driven to the secluded place to which horny teens had been drawn since before the paint on the incorporation sign for Earnest had dried.

"Christ," he murmured.

She laughed. "No. I think it's funny. I haven't been here since…"

He was pretty sure he knew the last time she'd been there. It probably coincided with the date of his last visit.

"God, look. There's two cars parked over there."

"Judging from the well-used path, I'm guessing the place still sees a lot of traffic."

"Especially since it seems it's a God-given right that all sixteen-year-olds own cars."

"And cell phones."

Her laugh made him remember exactly what they'd done the last time they were there.

And sparked in him a desire to revisit some old memories.

"Over there," she said, pointing to a favorite spot under an old oak tree.

He pulled in and turned off the engine, completely unprepared for the sexy assault Penelope instantly launched on his mouth…

PENELOPE WASN'T SURE what had come over her. One minute she'd been immersed in family problems—both hers and Palmer's—the next she was acting like an oversexed teen.

Perhaps dating on the sly was like riding a bike; once

you got back on, you instinctively knew where to put your feet.

Balance, on the other hand, was something else entirely.

She spread her fingertips over Palmer's stubble-peppered jaw, holding him still as she tasted his lips. Mmm…better than she remembered from even last night. Of course, then she'd been caught off guard, hadn't had a chance to register every last sensation. And she intended to do exactly that tonight. She wanted to savor every moment, commit it to memory so she might draw on it whenever she pleased.

The problem was, she couldn't seem to get close enough to him.

She scanned his side of the car.

"What are you looking for?" he asked.

"Doesn't the seat go back?"

"Back? *Oh*. Yes."

And just like that, a humming sounded and his seat began sliding backward.

"Mmm…much better."

Hiking up the skirt of her dress, she straddled him, glad for the wide, plush seats of the high-end car.

"Whoa…" Palmer murmured.

When she made to get off, he held her steady with two viselike hands on her hips.

She leaned in and kissed him. And kissed him again. "I think this thing with your father…"

He squinted at her in the dim light from the dash. "What?"

She popped open the first button on the front of her dress. "Keep at it. He won't be able to shut you out forever."

"Are you really talking about my dad while you're undressing?"

She smiled. "You can't do two things at the same time?"

"Walk and chew gum, yes. Make love and talk about my father...no."

She laughed as she shrugged out of the top of her dress, baring her bra-covered breasts.

She heard his hard swallow and began to say something.

"Shh," he said, placing his fingers lightly against her mouth. "Don't say another word about anything."

"Why?" she managed through his hand.

"Because the only sound I want to hear right now is the sound of you breathing..."

She shivered at the softly said words, holding his gaze for a long moment before leaning forward again and kissing him. This time leisurely. With sweet deliberation. Not unlike the car seat when he'd moved it back, she felt like she was humming, vibrating with anticipation of what was to come, yet reveling in each sensation that washed over her.

He reached up and cupped her right breast through her bra, sending heat winding through her like a red ribbon. He lightly pinched her nipple, bringing it to a stiff peak and then fastened his mouth over it, moisture penetrating the fabric of her bra. Remembering her underwear preferences, he pushed the cups upward and then the entire sports bra up and over her head, the elastic snapping as he tossed it to the other side of the car.

Penelope made a move to complain and then froze when she felt his mouth directly on her nipple.

Dear God in heaven...

His tongue made slow circles around her areola and then he suckled that über-sensitive bit of skin, the sensual act accelerating her heart rate and dampening her panties even further.

She pressed herself more firmly against him, feeling his hardness against her softness...and hungering to feel an even closer connection.

She reached between them, tugging his shirt from his pants, then dipping her fingertips inside the waist. She knew a little thrill when she instantly met with the burgeoning head. But there were too many clothes in the way!

She quickly undid his belt and popped the catch on his slacks, not stopping until she held his long, thick length against the palm of her hand.

Her mouth watered with the desire to taste him. But she didn't want to break the connection as he stroked and licked her breasts.

Instead, she pulled aside the drenched crotch of her panties and positioned him in her shallow channel.

She shuddered from head to foot.

Palmer groaned. "I'm not wearing protection," he said between clenched teeth.

She swallowed past her tight throat even as she shifted her hips, moving herself back and forth over him, her own juices lubricating the movement.

So hard...so hot...so good.

He grasped her hips. "Let me get a condom from my back pocket."

She jerked herself until the thick top of his arousal was positioned against her.

"You don't need it," she said, and slid down over him, taking him in inch by precious inch, feeling him stretching her filling her loving her.

13

THE SENSATION OF HAVING Penelope surround him, no clothes, no latex, nothing between them, was like emerging from the clouds to find a sun-drenched heaven.

Fire licked through his groin, coalescing in his aching balls as she shuddered around him.

He forgot where they were, what they had been talking about, lost in everything that was Penelope Weaver.

She shifted her hips, grinding her pelvis against his, the friction sending spiraling flames up into his chest. He felt like a powder keg with the fuse burning closer and closer. He tried to slow her movements to ward off climax, but she was having none of it. She kissed him soulfully, seeking an even deeper meeting. He could hear the hiss of the fuse and…

The beam of a flashlight cut across Penelope's beautiful face, following by a hard rapping of knuckles against the hood.

"Break it up in there," a familiar voice said.

PENELOPE FROZE. Not in crisis but in horror.

Barnaby...

Palmer helped her cover herself with her dress that was bunched around her hips, but she didn't dare to move so they remained joined, staring at the sheriff's shocked face through the open window.

"Aw, Christ..."

Barnaby snapped upright and then paced a ways away, cursing under his breath as he gave them some space.

"Oh, God." Penelope slid over to the passenger's seat, trying to find her bra, then giving up and doing up the front buttons of her dress. At least she was saved the humiliation of searching for her panties.

She straightened herself up and looked over at Palmer who only had to tuck himself back inside his pants and pull up the zipper and cinch his belt.

She closed her eyes tightly.

Please, please tell me this isn't happening....

Guilt and humiliation were two emotions she didn't want to feel on the heels of exquisite passion. But there they were. Laying waste to everything that had happened only minute before.

She drew in a deep breath and reached for the car door handle.

Palmer rested a hand on her arm. "You don't have to do this now."

She stared at him in the dark. "Yes, I do."

She climbed out of the car, but couldn't seem to bring her shaking legs to carry her around to the other side.

"Barnaby, please…"

He held his hand up, and then moved it to rub his eyes as if unable to bring himself to look at her directly. "The man's right, Penelope. It's not a good idea to do this now." He nodded toward the road. "You just go on home now. I'll…I'll…"

Talk to her later?

She felt like she wanted to be sick.

"I'll talk to you tomorrow," she said quietly. "I'm so sorry, Barnaby—"

He held up his hand again.

She got back into the car and Palmer started it, within moments putting the shaken sheriff out of sight.

While he had disappeared from view, Penelope was afraid the reality of the situation would never leave her.

LONG AFTER HE'D DROPPED Penelope off, Palmer sat in his car outside his father's house. He knew he should return to the B and B. Go over the list of people Manolis Philippidis had compiled for him to work with. Analyze which of them he could rely on to finally get this venture off the ground.

But all he could think about was the stricken expression on Penelope's face when they'd been caught at Makeout Cove. Remember how quiet she'd been on the drive back into town. He'd apologized for having played a rôle in the uncomfortable drama and she'd blinked at him, almost as if she'd forgotten he was there.

He rubbed his hands over his face, still smelling her there. His immediate physical reaction was painful. And not just in the sexual sense. A strange, almost restless ball of energy had settled in his solar plexus. As if Penelope had opened a hole inside him and filled it with her essence. Making it impossible to think of anything else but her.

And filling him with the overwhelming desire to seek out her company.

Movement in the house caught his attention. He refocused his attention on the front window where he could see his father sitting at his TV tray in front of the television. He watched as Thomas moved the tray, pointed the remote at the set to shut it off, then turned off the light.

Bedtime.

Palmer let his head fall back against the seat rest and a long breath hissed from between his teeth. What a pair they'd become. He and his old man were trapped in some sort of bubble. Boxed in by the choices they'd made in their lives, their options limited, their courses set.

Which made no sense at all to him. He'd returned to Earnest to forge a new path. Or maybe to find his way back to the old one and push ahead, using what he'd achieved while away to help not only himself, but the town.

WE
CAN GO
ANYWHERE
WE WANT

rGrannys

we can eo
tothe store
we can go tothe
park.byw

♡   ♡

Now he felt as powerless as that man inside the dark house.

He started the rental car and put it into gear, wishing it was as easy to do to his own life...

PENELOPE DROVE THE CAR she shared with her grandmother and great-aunt no more than once, twice a week. There was little need for her to do so. The shop was within walking distance, as was most everything else. The only time she used it was to do the weekly grocery shopping in nearby Chauncy. And run other errands that lay outside her walking range.

Like the errand she was on this morning.

Her hands grew damp on the steering wheel.

Stupid, stupid, stupid.

What had happened last night was nothing short of foolish to the nth degree. To run off to Makeout Cove with Palmer and act like she was a hormone-ridden teenager when she was a full-grown adult with adult responsibilities and considerations....

One of those to the man she was dating and who referred to himself as her boyfriend, even if she didn't.

She pulled up to the old filling station on the outskirts of town that had been transformed into the sheriff's office a decade or so ago. Three squad cars were parked in front bearing the sheriff's logo. She recognized the one on the far right as Barnaby's car. And considered turning around and heading straight back into town.

Coward, she called herself.

She parked and shut the old Pontiac off, wiping her palms against her simple cotton dress. This wasn't going to be easy. The mere memory of Barnaby's horror last night made her stomach churn.

She climbed out of the car and reached for the box on the passenger's seat, then stood staring at the front windows, although the slanting morning sunlight guaranteed she could see little than her own reflection. Her dark hair was frizzy from the humidity and her dress wilted against her body. Hot. It was still far too hot for Earnest, Washington. The local radio show had broadcast that there were storms heading their way that might break the heat wave, but then told residents not to hold their breath. After all, they hadn't seen the heat coming, so who could say with any amount of certainty when it might leave?

Penelope forced her feet toward to the door. She had little doubt that Barnaby knew she was there. Usually, he would have come out to meet her.

But not today.

Nor, she suspected, any other day.

The door opened outward as she neared it and Sam, one of the deputies smiled at her and the box she held.

"Morning, Penelope. Those aren't what I think they are?"

"If you're thinking they're blueberry muffins, then no, they're not."

He grimaced. "Damn."

She held the box out to him. "They're cranberry."

His grin returned as he accepted the baked goods and held them up so the other five employees on the other side of the low wall could see. "Breakfast!"

Penelope smiled and quietly accepted thanks even as her gaze strayed to the glassed-in office to her right. Barnaby appeared to be on the phone, but rather than sitting at his desk where he would be facing her, he stood facing away.

By design? She had little doubt.

She cleared her throat. That was okay. She supposed she deserved to be kept waiting at the very least.

At most...

She looked down at her sandals and her neon-pink painted nails.

"Penelope," Barnaby said.

She blinked up to find him standing in front of her without her realizing he had moved.

The office went quiet. She supposed if they didn't know what had happened last night, they had at least picked up on the change in temperature between the two of them. Barnaby's face was so long his jaw nearly dragged on the floor.

"Can I talk to you?" she asked.

His eyes narrowed. "Go ahead."

She looked around at the others in various stages of eating the muffins. "Outside?"

He didn't say anything for a long moment. And she figured it would be his due to insist she speak her piece here, in front of God and everyone.

Instead, he held his hand out toward the door. "After you."

Before the door closed after them, the conversation inside had returned to normal. Hopefully none of them would make things more difficult for Barnaby when he went back.

"Barnaby, I..." she began when they'd walked around to the side of the building where his car was parked.

When she didn't continue, he nodded and said, "You..."

"Last night..."

He visibly winced.

This wasn't going at all as she'd hoped. Then again, what had she expected? What she'd done was unforgivable.

Barnaby frowned. "I wouldn't say unforgivable," he said in response to the words she hadn't realized she'd said out loud. "Unforgettable, yes. Unforgivable..."

He seemed to mull over the situation.

"It wasn't right." Penelope wanted to reach out, touch his arm. He really was a good man. Tall, handsome, sweet. But the spark had somehow never materialized. She'd thought that was all right. It had been so long since she'd felt that passion that she really hadn't missed it. Although she had known something wasn't completely right between them. She viewed him as more brother material than lover.

And, perhaps, if he were being honest, the same applied to him.

She'd never tell him that, though. She figured that saying he was like a brother to her was akin to saying he was like a friend. And no man liked to hear that.

So she didn't make any explanation at all. She wasn't entirely clear on why she'd slept with Palmer...twice. And indulged in one really hot petting session.

Barnaby wouldn't want to hear the details. She'd come here to apologize for her less than stellar behavior. Nothing more.

The rest she'd have to work out on her own.

He nodded when she apologized. "I figure I knew the minute DeVoe rolled back into town that we'd end up standing where we are." He gave her a half grin. "I could have written the dialogue."

She dropped her gaze. "Well, then, you were way ahead of me. Because the last thing..."

She trailed off, coming a little too close to TMI territory.

She drew in a deep breath instead and smiled. "Well, then..."

They stood like that for long moments in the shade, both of them absorbing the past few minutes.

Then Penelope looked at her watch. "I'd better go open the shop."

"Were those muffins I spotted?" he asked.

"Yes. Although if you want one, you'd probably better get in there."

She led the way back to the front of the building, blinking at the full sunlight.

"Penelope?"

She faced where he stood in front of the station door.

"Be careful in that old jalopy. If I catch you speeding, I will ticket you."

She laughed, relieved at the return of the Barnaby of old.

"Do that, Sheriff, and risk never getting a free muffin again."

His grin was full. "Understood."

As she returned his warm smile, she hoped that they'd be able to salvage friendship out of the debris of their almost relationship.

"Goodbye, Barn," she said quietly.

"Goodbye, Penelope. And good luck."

She tucked her chin closer to her chest and nodded. Why did she have the feeling she was going to need it?

She got into her car and started it, giving him a final wave before pointing the grill back toward town.

14

"MEET ME AT THE DINER for lunch."

Palmer would have preferred the invitation had come from Penelope, but his old pal Caleb Payne came in at a close second. And after the morning from hell spent dealing with resistant suppliers, obnoxious foremen and a general sensation that nothing was ever going to move forward with his project, he could use a little steam-letting. Even if a beer at the pub sounded like a better bet.

He entered the Quality Diner for the first time since his return to town. He stopped just inside the door, feeling, for not the first time like he'd stepped fifteen years into the past. Very little had changed about the place. The walls were still painted a light violet. The tiles were still black and white. The white Formica tables were still paired with red leather booths. All that was missing was a soda jerk at the long counter at the back.

Caleb waved to him from the middle booth in front

of the window. He headed in that direction and shook his hand when he rose to his feet. They indulged in a man hug with their joined hands between them and then Palmer slid in the seat across from him.

"You look like hell," Caleb said.

Palmer grimaced at him. "Yes, well, I feel like hell."

Caleb, on the other hand, looked as put together as always. Even when they played a little one-on-one at a basketball court, the man appeared as if he'd just stepped out of the shower instead of in dire need of one.

He accepted a menu from a teenaged waitress. "So what brings you to town?"

When his friend didn't answer, he looked over the menu to find Caleb with his right brow cocked. "Are you still dating that Metaxas girl?"

Saying the name made Palmer remember his "chance" meeting with Troy at the pub a couple of days ago.

Caleb asked, "Is there a reason why I shouldn't be?"

He mentally made his choice and put the menu down. "The truth? She's too good for you."

Caleb's grimace was comical. The powerful business-man had rarely shown much emotion in all the time Palmer had known him. Steely gaze, threatening glare, even the occasional hearty chuckle, but never a facial expression more suited to their young waitress.

"I know. I tell myself that every morning when I get up, and every night when I go to bed."

Palmer squinted at him. "Are you serious?"

"Deadly."

There. That was the Caleb with whom he was more familiar. "What happened to, 'She knows the score. No one needs to get hurt so long as we stick to the ol' Caleb formula for dating'?"

He shifted on the booth, indicating a discomfort that was even more at odds than the grimace. "Yeah, well. Somehow no formula seems to fit when it comes to Miss Bryna Metaxas."

"So invent a new one."

"That's what I'm doing. I drive down here at least twice a week." He cursed under his breath. "I'm beginning to wonder if her cousins will ever accept me as her suitor, given my past connection to Philippidis."

"Past?"

"Definitely past." He picked up his coffee cup. "I want nothing to do with that old prick."

"That should help in the Metaxas department."

"You think?" He shook his head. "Then why do I still get the feeling that if I let my guard down, they'll take me out back for a good, old-fashioned whooping?"

"Because you're screwing their younger cousin."

"I've never screwed anything in my life."

It was Palmer's turn to cock a brow.

"I've fucked." Caleb waggled a finger. "But never screwed."

Palmer chuckled as he turned his coffee cup upright

and accepted a fill from the passing waitress. "I'm not sure the many women in your past would agree with that."

"Yes, well, that's their problem. Not mine."

The waitress put the coffeepot down on the table and turned the page on her order pad. "Today's specials are homemade meat loaf and mashed potatoes with gravy, an open-faced roast beef sandwich and minestrone soup."

Caleb opted for the soup, Palmer the meat loaf.

They talked about secondary issues until their food arrived. The weather, basketball, pre-season football and Caleb's mother, who, much to his chagrin, seemed to be spending an awful lot of time in Seattle lately.

Caleb sat back. "I mean, rare is when I see her more than twice in one year. I've seen her three times in the past month."

"I thought you two were close."

"We are. But not that close." He shook his head. "And she still won't tell me the name of the guy she's seeing."

"Ah."

"What do you mean by, 'ah'?"

"You think this may have to do with her spending so much time with someone else?"

Caleb stared at him. "Christ, Palmer, I'm thirty-three, not twelve."

He chuckled. "Since when does age have anything to do with anything?"

"Since I graduated from middle school and passed puberty." He sipped his black coffee. "I'm not used to a hands-on mother, that's all. And since she's here, she's decided to take a more involved approach."

"That's good. Isn't it?"

Caleb stared at him again.

"Okay, then, maybe it's not."

Their food arrived and they dug in. Caleb added salt and pepper to his minestrone while Palmer spread the tomato sauce on top of the meat loaf around with his fork.

"So," Caleb said after a while. "Have you had it with Philippidis yet?"

Palmer slowed his chewing, the great meat loaf suddenly a handful of dried breadcrumbs in his mouth. "What?"

"You heard me. Has the old man made you hate him yet?"

"I've never had a problem with Manolis."

"Until…" Caleb led.

"Until I went into direct business with him." He sighed and tried the potatoes, which were also great. He added pepper. "I mean, I've partnered with him in the past, but my role was always limited."

"And now that you're in full partnership…your role is still limited."

"To the point of revolt."

Caleb grinned. "It's interesting that you don't see any long-term employees around the Greek, don't you think?"

"I'm not following you."

"Think about it. Every man who's been in business for a while has at least one or two dedicated, loyal men or women in their employ. Someone who's been with him for years. Since the beginning."

"But not Philippidis."

"Right."

His friend had a point. Back in Boston, Palmer had three men he relied on and trusted implicitly, their friendship cemented at college, their working relationship solidified through the first tough couple of years. Each may have gone on to work on projects of their own, but they'd never completely dissolved the original partnership.

Then there was him and Caleb. Even though their business relationships were of a temporary nature, they always remained friends.

He couldn't think of one person he could say the same for with Philippidis.

"The guy talks a good game in the beginning," Caleb continued. "Lures you in with his charm and vision."

Palmer listened intently.

"Then shortly after you sign on the dotted line, he lowers the boom, his need to control and manipulate ruining whatever good foundation was originally created."

Palmer frowned. His meal was good, but he was increasingly losing his appetite.

"So, I'll repeat my question. Have you had it with Philippidis yet?" his friend asked.

"No. But I'm coming close."

Caleb finished his soup and wiped his mouth with his paper napkin. "Well, when you get there, give me a call. I have a few ideas in mind I think may interest you."

"Why not propose them now?"

Caleb grinned. "No. I need you to be good and pissed before I swing these by you." He got up from the table, peeling off enough bills to cover lunch for everyone in the diner. "Come on, let's go. Bryna's waiting for me back at the house." He chuckled quietly. "It's the only time we can be alone when I'm here."

Palmer held up his hand. "Spare me the details."

"I will. But only because I know you have a few details of your own you haven't shared with me yet."

Palmer led the way outside, stopping on the sidewalk. "What do you mean?"

"Oh, no. That's not for me to say. You have to make a shot for the basket before I go for the rebound, old friend."

They did the man-hug thing again and then Caleb headed for his sports car parked up the block.

Palmer stood there for long moments, pondering his friend's words. Then he shook his head and walked toward his own car.

PENELOPE CLOSED UP THE SHOP early that afternoon
and headed home, the heat and slow day combining to
make it impossible for her to be alone with her thoughts
any longer. She hoped a good, strong dose of humor-
ous reality from her grandmother and aunt would be
just the thing she needed to get her riotous emotions
under control.

She let herself into the house only to find it empty.

Great. They must be working.

She sighed and hung her purse, patting Thor on the
head when he happily greeted her with a wet nose to
the inside of her knee, then she walked to the kitchen
and poured herself a tall glass of homemade lemonade
with lots of ice. She supposed she could switch on the
air conditioning, but she couldn't bring herself to.

Instead, she let the dog out back and then followed
him, sitting down on the top of the porch steps.

How many times had she sat in this exact same spot,
pondering the world at large and Palmer in specific? She
sipped the lemonade and pulled her hair back from her
damp neck with her free hand.

This wasn't working. This…whatever it was.

The thought had been going through her head all
day after she'd gone to see Barnaby that morning. And
it refused to budge.

Of course, to do anything about it, she first had to
define what "this" was.

So Palmer DeVoe was back in town. And the minute

he'd come back, she'd suddenly turned into a starry-eyed teen with nothing more to worry about than planning clandestine meetings with her boyfriend in the cornfield.

Thor did his business and came to sit on the sidewalk at her feet, panting.

She put her glass down and got the hose, filling his outdoor bowl with fresh water. He sloshed it everywhere, splashing her feet in the process as she reseated herself on the steps.

It had been a long time since she was a teenager. She'd be better off remembering that.

So why was it that every time she saw Palmer, all she wanted to do was strip off her panties and climb on top of him?

"No sex life," she said aloud.

She pulled her hair back again and fashioned it into a twist to get it off her neck and then pulled at the front of her dress to encourage a breeze. Whether the thin sheen of sweat that coated her skin was due to the weather or her thoughts of Palmer—or a combination of both—she didn't know. But she did know that she didn't want to cool off.

Not yet.

But there would come a time when she'd have to end it. When she'd have to finally tell him what she was keeping secret. The information that made it crystal clear that she had stopped being a teenager a long, long time ago. Leaving her absolutely amazed that she could still feel the way she was, considering.

In the meantime, she intended to lap up every last drop that she could.

15

PALMER OPENED THE rusty-hinged doors to the maintenance shed in the backyard of his father's house. The grass was so high he had to work the left door so it could move.

After telling the work crew they might as well go home since they weren't doing anything anyway, he'd gone to the B and B, changed into shorts and a T-shirt and athletic shoes, then headed to his father's house to find the doors shut tight.

How could the old man stand it in there without air-conditioning? Not even a window was cracked, probably to prevent him any access to the place at all.

He did, however, still remember the combination to the lock on the shed. And now stood staring at a mower that was almost as old as he was.

He eyed the ancient machine, then put on the work gloves he'd bought before pulling the thing out.

"You're not going to get that heap to work," someone called out.

He looked over to see one of the neighbors contemplating him from her back deck, her arms crossed over her chest.

"Palmer? God, is that you?"

The arms came down and the woman crossed the yard and stopped at the chain-link fence separating her yard from his dad's.

"It's Cindy Hess. Remember? You and I used to play doctor in that very shed when we were five."

Palmer looked into the cramped shed, searching for the memory. While he couldn't find that one in particular, he did recall the pretty redhead who epitomized the term "girl next door."

She was just as pretty, but she was no longer a redhead but a blonde.

"There was a time when I thought you and I might... well, you know, end up together." She looked toward the house where there were sounds of children arguing over something. "Then you met Penelope Weaver and any chance I may have had flew north not just for the summer, but forever."

Palmer took in the neat lawn, the kiddy pool and the beagle chained to the deck. "Looks like you didn't do too badly."

She followed his gaze and shrugged. "I guess. I married Joe Johnson. We have three kids and bought this place from my parents six years ago." She squinted at him. "God, I heard you were back in town. And Joe said he thought he saw you over here the other day, but he couldn't be sure."

"Yes, it's me. I thought I'd come over and do some yard work."

"You staying at Foss's B and B?"

"Is there anyplace else?"

She laughed. "No." She gestured toward the mower. "Like I said, you're not going to cut anything with that except your line to reality. Your father hasn't used it in years. He used to pay my older boy, Bill, to care for the lawn, but then Bill graduated to a paper route and stopped cutting grass."

Palmer unscrewed the gas cap to find the well bone-dry.

"You can you use ours if you like," Cindy offered.

"You sure?"

"Of course, I'm sure." Her green eyes sparkled in the sunlight. "What good are neighbors if not for borrowing mowers and playing doctor in the shed?"

Within minutes, he'd collected the borrowed mower from Cindy's garage, met two of her three kids, and was back at his dad's place. The grass was so high, the mower stalled several times while he was doing the front yard. He moved to the back...and walked straight into a full spray of water.

"Shit!"

He released his hold on the mower and it sputtered off. He held his arm up, allowing him to see that the water was coming from a hose...a hose his father had aimed at him from the back steps.

"Get out my yard, boy!" the old man shouted.

Palmer stared at him for long moments, then followed the hose as it snaked around the house on one side. He shut off the faucet then stalked back around to face his father again.

Thomas DeVoe shook the hose a couple of times, disgusted. Then he made for the side of the house, presumably to turn the water back on.

As he came back, Palmer picked up a middle section of the hose and twisted it. "And if you find a way around that, I'll turn off the water source entirely." The old man glared at him. "You forget, I used to live here."

"But not anymore."

To Palmer's surprise, his father advanced on him.

He took a step back, releasing his hold on the hose... allowing his father to turn it on him full blast.

He sputtered at the force then rushed the old man. They struggled for the hose with first one then the other getting the full onslaught. Palmer noticed that Cindy had come out of the house along with another woman and openly watched them, and on the sidewalk in front of the house, another couple had stopped.

His father got the upper hand again and hit him full in the face.

"Jesus!"

He finally wrestled the hose from his hands and backed up, trying to figure out a way to shut the damn thing off. His father advanced. He backed up and sprayed his milky-white shins.

"Don't even think about it."

"Give me back that goddamn hose."

"Not a chance in hell." He gestured toward the back door. "Now go on and get back inside. And fix us something for dinner."

"I already ate."

Palmer stared at him even as he found the mechanism that locked the sprayer in place. The water ceased. "Well, I haven't. So make something for me. I'm going to be plenty hungry once I finish."

"Don't you touch that yard."

Palmer rolled the hose up and hung it over the faucet at the side of the house. "Sorry to disappoint you, Pops, but I already did. It's more than half done."

He stood some ten feet away from the old man.

"Unless you feel up to doing it?"

Thomas didn't say anything. Merely stared at him. And then he stalked back inside the house. The slamming of the door made everyone watching jump. Including Palmer.

After long moments, he finally turned back toward the mower. "Sorry about that," he called out to the neighbors.

They waved and disappeared one by one.

He turned the mower back on...

PENELOPE GOT UP TO CLEAR the kitchen table of dinner dishes. Since she'd arrived home first, she'd decided to make chicken with mac and cheese, surprising her grandmother and great-aunt when they'd come home from cleaning an office in nearby Chauncy.

"That was a nice surprise," her aunt said, sitting back in her chair.

Agatha sipped at her iced tea. "Very nice. You should come home early more often, Penelope."

Throughout dinner, conversation had naturally centered on the weather and the impact it was having on the garden and area farmers, not to mention their electric bill. Penelope had switched the air on before cooking so she wouldn't melt along with the cheese.

But now that they had finished, she felt her roommates' gazes on her, perhaps looking a little too closely.

"So…" her grandmother began. "Did you have a nice rest last night?"

Penelope's movements slowed as she spooned fresh fruit salad into bowls and placed them on the table. "Why, yes. Yes, I did. Thanks for asking."

Her aunt accepted a clean spoon. "No more headaches?"

Against her better judgment, Penelope sat down. "No."

Her grandmother nodded as she ate a bite of pineapple. "So you wouldn't happen to know a thing about what happened at Makeout Cove last night, would you?"

Irene faked a surprised look. "She was resting in

her room with a headache. How could she possibly know?"

"Oh...maybe because she was there?"

Penelope gave an eye roll. "Oh, for Pete's sake, just get on with it. What do you want to know?"

Her aunt actually scooted her chair a little closer to the table. "Were you really with that Palmer DeVoe?"

"Did poor Barnaby really come across you?" This from her grandmother.

"Yes. And yes."

The two older women waited.

"Look, I'm not going to say anything more on the matter, okay?" She moved her fruit around, but didn't eat any. "I'm having a hard enough time accepting everything myself."

"So that's why you wanted the extra muffins this morning," her grandmother ventured.

"I took a box by the station so I could talk to Barnaby."

Her aunt shook her head. "The boy is too good for the likes of you."

Penelope's jaw fell open. "What?"

"I disagree," her grandmother said. "But I understand that point she's trying to make. To lead one guy on while doing another..." She shook her head.

"Let me guess. Skank."

Agatha smiled. "You said it, not me."

"Look, I never slept with Barnaby."

"But you never told him you wouldn't, which meant he had hope that you might."

"How many times have you slept with Palmer since he's been back?" Irene interrupted.

Penelope held her hand up. "This is where this conversation ends."

"No, girl," her grandmother said sternly. "This is exactly where it begins."

She had been prepared to abandon her spot at the table, but now sat tight.

"How did he take the news?" Agatha asked.

Penelope dropped her gaze to the table, wishing she could crawl inside the bowl of fruit and hide behind a grape. Something, anything to spare her from this.

"You didn't tell him," her great-aunt said. She looked at her grandmother. "She didn't tell him."

"I know she didn't tell him. Because if she had told him, she wouldn't have fixed us dinner tonight. Or tomorrow night. Or any other night in the near future. She'd be closed up in her room for real, crying her eyes out."

"Just like she did fifteen years ago. You remember? We barely saw her for a month."

"Do I remember? How can I forget? I practically had to hand-feed a nineteen-year-old who refused to eat."

On top of everything that had occurred in the past week, she didn't really need to be reminded of this.

Then again, she didn't need reminding, period. Because it was there. Just below the surface. Behind her every thought, every action.

Her grandmother leveled a no-nonsense gaze at her. "When are you going to tell the man that he has a son?"

16

PALMER FINISHED MOWING, trimming and seeing to some of the more pressing landscaping problems and after returning borrowed materials, and hauling bags of clippings to the curb, he washed up at the very hose that had soaked him earlier, with his father's help. Einstein's theory of relativity held special importance as he enjoyed the feel of the cold water on his face now. Earlier...

Well, earlier, the spray had been an affront.

He shut off the water and shook his hands dry and wiped his face. He'd do a better job inside, but this would do for now.

He walked around to the back of the house. The door was closed.

Palmer frowned. He wasn't surprised. Apparently his father had shut himself back up inside.

Just out of curiosity, he tried the screen door. Open.

He hesitated on the inner door. What would he do this time if it were locked?

He stretched his neck, looking over his shoulder at the neatly cut lawn, then turning back toward the door with its square window covered on the inside with yellow curtains. He curved his hand around the knob and took a deep breath...and easily turned it.

His heart beat an uneven rhythm. Had the old man overlooked locking it? He'd taken the time to close both doors. Why not lock them? Habit?

He stepped inside the kitchen to complete silence... to find a plate of peanut butter and jelly sandwiches cut and waiting on the kitchen table.

Palmer stood in the middle of the room and rubbed his chin, fighting a smile.

Finally. Progress...

WHILE PALMER MIGHT BE forced to accept incremental steps forward in his estranged relationship with his father, on the job site he was used to things progressing a little more expeditiously.

Inside the site trailer the following morning, he paced behind the nondescript metal desk that matched the metal filing cabinets and metal chairs with green pads. The bare windows were doing nothing to halt the heat, the air conditioning unit working overtime to keep the small space cool.

He moved the telephone receiver from his right ear to

his left. "What do you mean the order's been cancelled? I made no such request."

"I'm sorry, sir, but someone contacted us with all the relevant information."

Palmer rubbed his closed eyelids. "What's the name on the authorization?"

He wasn't surprised to find it belonged to Manolis Philippidis's secretary.

"Would you like us to reinstate the order, sir?"

He paused for a second, considering his options. "No. Not right now. Thank you. I'll call back after I've gotten a few answers."

He dropped the receiver back into the cradle as the trailer door swung open.

"DeVoe, we've got a problem out here."

He considered the new foreman. Of course they had a problem. The entire site was one big problem after another.

Grabbing his cell phone from the desktop, he followed the man outside. His steps slowed when he spotted the collection of workmen hanging around a forklift.

"What's going on, guys?" he asked.

The one he chose to focus on, who appeared to be the group leader, took a long sip of coffee from a thermos cup before responding. "Equipment failure, boss. We're not going to be able to do anything until it's repaired."

Palmer looked around. "There's plenty to do without the equipment."

"We can't do anything until we get all the materials on site."

Christ. At every turn, he was running head-on into roadblocks.

"Fine. No sense in hanging around here, then. Go home." He glanced at the foreman. "Get someone over here to fix this."

"It's going to take a couple of days."

"What?"

"The guy's gotta come down from Seattle."

"Don't be ridiculous. There's a shop on the other side of town."

He shrugged. "I was instructed to use this guy in particular, boss."

He didn't need to ask by whom.

"Fine. Get on it and get back to me with the timeline." He stalked back to the trailer and slammed the door, locking it behind him for good measure.

Was it really so short a time ago that he'd been on top of the world? That he'd enjoyed a measure of success that few men achieved in their lifetimes, much less before the age of thirty-five? That he'd taken on this venture to give back to a town he'd abandoned, to leave a legacy that hadn't been important to him until now? That he'd expected complete success?

Now, he felt as if his feet were mired in mud to the ankles, making each step not just a labor, but sometimes a physical impossibility. Roadblocks and dead ends faced him wherever he looked. And that old sensation of suffocation was beginning to creep into his dreams and haunt him throughout his waking hours.

He blinked, movement catching his eyes. He watched through the windows as the men he'd been "assigned" by Philippidis left one by one in their trucks and cars, abandoning a site that was only a job to them. And one they apparently didn't relish performing.

For Palmer, it was a chance to prove himself on a level that his outside successes had never risen to.

He scanned the drafting table and the design plans there. The hard hat and tool belt. The filing cabinets filled with paperwork and contracts that had either been voided or soon would be.

And there didn't appear to be a damn thing he could do about it.

Or was there?

Ordering his feet into action, he grabbed his car keys from the hook near the door and walked back outside.

It was time to straighten this mess out once and for all…

PENELOPE, ON THE OTHER HAND, was having a very busy day when all she wanted was quiet to think about what she had to do.

But it seemed everybody and their sister had heard about what had happened at Makeout Cove and wanted to ferret out the details firsthand.

Details Penelope wasn't about to share. Worse, every

time someone brought it up, she cringed all over again at the abuse Barnaby must be suffering.

How had something private gone so very public?

She served coffee for the umpteenth time, a smile carefully affixed to her face.

"Is it true what they say, Penelope?" Jenny Hansen asked as she lingered at the counter, slowly adding sugar to her small coffee. "Did Barnaby really catch you and Palmer DeVoe going at it at Makeout Cove?"

Penelope offered up a smile she'd spent the past two hours practicing. "Oh, Jen, you know better than to ask such a question. Considering the hours you and Johnny spent up there...well, what happens at Makeout Cove stays at Makeout Cove."

Her old classmate laughed, but didn't seem to appreciate the mention of her onetime high school sweetheart, now ex-husband. She dug in her heels, as if she didn't intend to cede the point, when a white-haired man in a neatly ironed lime-green shirt and brown pants elbowed his way in front of the counter...and forced Jenny to move out.

Penelope gave him a brief smile of thanks, then hoped that he didn't plan to pursue the same line of questioning. She was an inch away from chasing everyone out and turning around the Closed sign.

"Do you have anything that won't disagree too terribly with an old man's constitution?" he asked.

Then she realized who he was. Mr. Turner, her old high school English teacher who had been ancient back then. Now, he looked barely able to hold himself up, but did so with the help of two canes. It had been a while since she'd seen him. But he was a very welcome sight indeed.

"Good morning, Mr. Turner. I think I can find something," she said, helping him toward a chair in the corner. "Cranberry juice okay?"

"Actually, I've already had my daily cranberry. What else you got?"

She ran through a list of juices and sodas she had on hand.

"Actually, the coffee smells awfully good. Do you have any decaf?"

"I sure do."

She went back behind the counter, wishing the busyness of the day were due to the town being back on track instead of people wanting to gossip. At least she expected to have a good day receipt-wise as several people currently milled around, appearing satisfied to talk amongst themselves, likely sharing whatever little tidbits they'd gotten individually in order to weave their own tapestry of what had happened last night. She told herself that at least they appeared to be enjoying their coffees as they considered her own, real tapestries for sale on her walls. Still, she knew that tomorrow morning she'd go back to her normal quiet days filling internet orders.

Which might be both a blessing and a curse.

She served Mr. Turner his coffee and waited as he took a sip.

"Mmm. I haven't had a coffee that good in years. Thank you."

"You're very welcome."

Another couple of women came into the shop and she excused herself to go wait on them.

"Shame about what's happening to that DeVoe boy, don't you think?" Mr. Turner said.

Penelope's footsteps slowed. "Pardon me?"

For a moment, she experienced a shock of fear that Barnaby had done something, taken out a bit of revenge. But she quickly discounted that. Barnaby would never abuse the power of his position that way. It just wasn't in him.

"The business. He sent everybody home today."

She asked the newest visitors to have a look around, she'd be with them in a minute.

She squinted at Mr. Turner. "I'm not sure I understand."

She knew that Palmer had been stressed over the progress—or lack thereof—on the building site. But he'd given her very few details. And considering the weight of her own secret, she hadn't asked.

"That Greek guy...his partner," Mr. Turner said. "He keeps cutting him off at the knees."

Penelope didn't know any of this. And felt badly that she didn't. Then again, she'd never much indulged in gossip. Not when she'd been the target of so much of it while growing up. First with her unconventional family—her grandmother and aunt were legends in their own time—then with the questions that had surrounded Palmer's leaving and her own brief disappearance fifteen years ago.

Mr. Turner said, "Everything he does, the Greek undermines."

"How do you know this?" Penelope asked.

"My grand-nephew was on the first crew DeVoe hired…and then let go. He and the others have their ears to the ground, hoping things will change." He shook his head. "But it doesn't look like they're going to any time soon. Word has it even DeVoe himself left today."

Penelope's stomach dropped to somewhere down around her feet.

"Left?"

"Yes. The site is abandoned."

She drew in a deep breath. That didn't mean he'd left town. Did it?

"Are you okay?" Mr. Turner asked, looking as if he was going to struggle to his feet to assist her.

She laid her hand on his shoulder to still him. "I'm fine. Really."

"I'm sorry. I didn't mean to upset you."

She tried for a smile but failed miserably. "Why should hearing about Palmer DeVoe's work woes upset me?"

Mr. Turner's eyes were a little too intense. "Because he's left you before, hasn't he?"

"Excuse me, Penelope? We'd like to place our orders now, please?"

She turned to find her latest visitors standing back in front of the service counter.

"If you'll excuse me…" she said to Mr. Turner.

"By all means." He held up his cup. "This really is great coffee."

"Thank you."

17

PALMER DIDN'T WASTE MUCH TIME. He drove straight to Seattle and headed for the high-rise building that housed Philippidis's main headquarters. It was hard to believe it was only a few weeks ago that he'd come to the Pacific Northwest with high expectations and solid plans. Almost impossible to see at all through the debris of the present.

He took the elevator to the top floor, where he was mildly surprised to see that Caleb's old office still stood empty, and continued on to the suite at the end of the hall Philippidis called his Seattle home.

"Mr. DeVoe," his secretary said, immediately getting to her feet.

Her desk stood impressively in the middle of the big open lobby, a few smaller offices off to his right holding her assistants, the ceiling-to-floor windows to his left perfectly framing the city's skyline.

He mumbled something he hoped resembled a hello

and made for Philippidis's double office doors behind her desk.

"He's not in," she said, coming to stand before him to block his access.

Palmer easily rounded her and opened the doors inward with such force they slammed against the inside walls.

The office was empty.

"I just told you that he wasn't in."

He stared at her. "But he is in town."

"Yes. Shall I call him—"

"No. But if you're really interested in helping, you can tell me where he is."

She appeared to ponder the request, but he fully expected her to protect her longtime boss at all costs.

Instead, she surprised him by saying, "He's having a late lunch at Reynaldo's."

PALMER WAS FACED WITH A DECISION: Either go to the restaurant and confront Manolis Philippidis in public, possibly ending in a showdown, or wait for him at his office, where the secretary insisted he was due to return afterward.

He'd done so much waiting lately, he decided on the former.

"Sir, do you have a reservation?" a stuffy concierge asked him when he entered the posh hotel eatery.

"No," he admitted. "But I am expected."

He scanned the room and spotted the wealthy Greek in a far corner booth.

"There's my party now."

"Sir, I'll take you—"

But Palmer was already on his way.

He advanced on the table, Philippidis's gregarious laughter assaulting his ears as he neared. He was dining with a woman, but Palmer paid her little mind. Just another in a long line the Greek was using to ease the pain of his fiancée's betrayal, more than likely.

"Manolis," he said, stopping in front of the table. "We need to speak. Now."

The man at the table blinked at him, apparently so engrossed in his conversation with his date that it took him a minute to register Palmer and his words. Of course, the fact that the last person he probably expected to see there demanding a word was Palmer. He was supposed to be an hour away dealing with the piles of shit Manolis kept throwing his way.

"Palmer!" While the Greek's mouth smiled and his welcome was loud, his eyes made it obvious that he did not appreciate his appearance or his interruption. "Sit, sit," he said.

He motioned to a waiter and a chair was produced for Palmer to sit on. He considered rejecting it. Then decided otherwise when he realized every eye on the place was on them. No matter how much he'd love to ream Philippidis for what he'd done, he wanted answers first. And he wasn't going to get them if he launched right into his criticisms.

The Greek leaned forward, folding his hands on top of the table, giving Palmer his full attention. "Tell me, what is so important that it couldn't wait until we were back at the office?"

"Do I really have to outline the problem?" Palmer asked, attempting to gain control over his racing pulse.

Philippidis looked at his date and then back again. "I'm afraid you're going to have to, because I don't have a clue why you're so upset."

A waiter appeared to take his order. Palmer moved to wave him away, but was stopped by the sound of a woman's voice.

"Please, bring Mr. DeVoe the special," she instructed the waiter. "He looks like he could use a good meal."

Palmer looked at her for the first time, realizing with a start that he knew her.

It was Caleb's mother, Phoebe.

"Hello, Palmer," she said with a warm smile.

Christ. What in the hell was she doing with Philippidis? Laughing with the son of a bitch in a private booth in the back of an exclusive restaurant?

Then it dawned on him. Manolis Philippidis must be the man responsible for Phoebe Payne's frequent visits to Seattle recently.

Considering Caleb's own issues with the wealthy

businessman, Palmer suspected his friend was going to be none too happy about the personal association.

"Phoebe," Manolis said, taking her hand and kissing the back of it. The intimate gesture made Palmer's stomach lurch. "Could you please see if the rest facilities are as tasteful as the remainder of the restaurant and come back to tell me? Mr. DeVoe and I should have concluded our business by then."

Phoebe looked doubtful.

Palmer nodded.

"Very well then." She kissed Manolis on the cheek and then rose from the table. Conditioned from long years of tradition, Palmer stood as well, trading cheek kisses with her. She hesitated, holding his gaze, as if asking him not to report what he'd seen to her son.

Palmer raised a brow, not about to keep such an important secret.

Finally, she moved out of view and he retook his seat, facing the man directly responsible for almost every sleepless moment he'd had over the past few weeks.

Palmer noticed that all pretense had left the Greek's face now that his date was no longer there to witness the exchange.

"What in the hell do you think you're doing?" he demanded.

"Funny, that was going to be my question to you," Palmer said. "But you know what? I no longer need to ask it. Because I'm done. This. You. Me. This sham of a business deal. Over."

"I advise you to read the fine print in our contract, Mr. DeVoe."

"With all due respect, I'd advise you to go to hell, Mr. Philippidis."

The waiter arrived with his food. He indicated that Manolis should have it and left the restaurant.

TWO DAYS LATER, Penelope sat on the back steps staring at the back yard as she absently aimed a hose at the wilting garden. Nearly three weeks without rain. It was virtually unheard of in Washington State. She unwittingly hit Thor with the spray and he barked and then ran around it to the other side, his aversion to water forgotten in the heat.

She hadn't heard from Palmer. Not that she expected to. Curiosity had gotten the better of her yesterday and she'd stopped by the bed-and-breakfast and asked to leave a message. Debra Foss, the owner, had informed her that he'd checked out two days earlier.

He'd left without saying anything.

She pushed her damp hair back from her face with her free hand. At least he'd given her the simple courtesy of saying goodbye fifteen years ago. She'd known exactly down to the minute when he would be leaving town in his old Dodge. And had known for nearly six months prior to his departure. Three months before she'd discovered she was pregnant with their child.

A hot tear trickled down her cheek and she slowly wiped it away. She didn't know why she should feel so raw now. She'd lived with the painful memories for so long, they were second nature to her.

Perhaps it was his leaving again that had reopened the wound. Compelled her to revisit emotions she had long tucked under her pillow and never looked at again. Lord knew she'd revisited so many of the other memories. Temptation…passion…love.

She swallowed hard. Yes, she realized, she loved him. Had never stopped loving him. He'd been her first…well, everything. And at the time she'd expected he'd be her last. She'd just had no idea it would be this way.

To fall in love with him and lose him all over again was the cruelest of fates. And perhaps exactly what she deserved.

Thor barked again and she heard the hinges on the screen door squeak as someone came outside. Her grandmother sat down next to her.

"We should turn on the air inside, but somehow I just can't bring myself to do it."

Penelope nodded.

"If only more of life's problems could be fixed by flipping a switch or turning a knob."

She released the lever and the water cut off. Thor gave a mighty shake and then trotted up to sit in front of her, panting.

"I heard the news," her grandmother said quietly.

"Oh?" She decided to play dumb.

"Irene and I stopped by Thomas DeVoe's house today."

Penelope squinted at her. "What would you two want at Palmer's father's place?"

Her grandmother smiled. "I don't know if you've noticed, but single men our age are few and far between here in Earnest." She shrugged her shoulders. "We decided to get a look at Thomas up close and personal. I mean, we've seen him at church every now and again, but not close up for years."

"And?"

"And he told us his son left again."

At least Palmer had spoken to his father. "That's not what I meant."

"I know. But we're going to stick to my topic, not be diverted by yours. You're not nearly as good at it as I am."

Penelope grimaced. "I'll take that as a compliment."

"You would."

She took a deep breath, the scent of cold water on hot cement filling her senses. "Mom called earlier."

"I heard. You told her?"

"Told her what?"

"That Palmer left again."

"I never told her he was back."

"Of course not. Why do that? Then you'd have to admit you were seeing him."

"I wasn't seeing him."

"No, you were just having monkey sex with him."

Penelope bit her tongue.

"Anyway, your mother's caught up in her own

dilemma at the moment. Hell, what am I talking about? She's always caught up in her own little dramas."

She smiled.

"You know, Betty was never mother material."

Penelope slanted her a look. "Must run in the family."

Her grandmother winced and she immediately felt guilty.

"I'm sorry...I..."

Agatha reached over and took her hand, pulling it over until it sat on her knee. "Look, Penelope, I know that you've got to be thinking about the past a lot. Hauling it back up to the present."

She concentrated on Thor.

"I just wanted to tell you, it's not the same."

It was exactly the same.

Then again, maybe it wasn't. Because at least Palmer had said goodbye back then. Now...

"I never got the chance to tell him," she confessed without intending to.

She felt her grandmother's gaze on her profile.

"He's gone, and again, he doesn't know."

"You understand that it's the twenty-first century?"

She looked at her.

"There's the invention of the cell phone. Computers. A whole slew of ways to find or contact someone. Used to be a person could drop off the edge of the earth. Not anymore. Wherever they go, they leave a digital trail."

Penelope didn't say anything.

"You want me to find him?"

She laughed without humor. "For what?"

"So you can tell him."

"Because he deserves to know," she said, nodding her head.

"No." Her grandmother appeared slightly surprised. "Because you deserve to have help shouldering the responsibility you've born alone all these years."

18

It took Palmer three days to work out the legal logistics involved with breaking the contract with Philippidis. He put his head together with his Seattle attorneys, working late into the night, returning to his hotel room spent and numb.

But, finally, he was free. Or as free as he was going to get. There might be some more legal haggling down the road, and Philippidis reserved the right to sue him, but his attorneys had found a couple of narrow loopholes, and even managed to work up an argument that couples used to annul a marriage.

He'd gotten an annulment.

The terminology amused Palmer, even as he tried to shake off the residue that had built up over the past few days.

He'd picked up the phone to call Penelope on several occasions, but decided to wait to talk to her when he got back to Earnest. No matter how much he ached to hear her voice or share his news with her, he'd wanted to make sure everything was taken care of first.

One favorable aspect of his stay was Caleb Payne. Seeing as his friend also had a woman in Earnest that he didn't see nearly as much as he wanted to, he had plenty of time to catch a meal, a beer and a pickup game of b-ball.

"You still can't shoot for shit," Caleb told him, easily grabbing the basketball after his misfire.

Palmer guarded him, the rubber soles of their shoes squeaking against the polished wood floor at Caleb's club. He threw his hands up to the right…Caleb shot from the left.

"All net."

"Glad something's going right in your life," Palmer taunted.

Caleb stopped cold in the middle of the court and he charged the hoop unchallenged.

"Top that."

His friend accepted the ball, but rather than dribbling it, he stood staring at him. "Come again."

Palmer wiped the sweat from his brow with the back of his wrist. "I told you to top that."

Caleb gestured with his free hand. "Before that."

"What? About something going well in your life?"

"Yes. That would be it."

Palmer straightened. "Just something to throw you off. All's fair in love and basketball."

Caleb's eyes narrowed.

Damn. Palmer should have known better than to toss that little throwaway comment his friend's way. Caleb had a way of getting to the bottom of anything he set his mind to.

There was no way he was going to be the bearer of the bad news about his mother dating Manolis Philippidis. The way he saw it, he was saving his friend from life imprisonment. Because once Caleb found out, he would surely kill the Greek.

"No. There's more to it than that." His frown was dark and it was obvious that he wasn't going to continue the game until he got some answers.

Palmer took the ball from him.

"Is it something with Bryna? The Metaxas brothers?"

He shot and hit, but there was little reward without Caleb's participation. "What? No. Of course not."

"What is it then?"

Palmer chuckled uneasily. He'd opened the can of worms. He was just going to have to serve them up as appetizingly as possible. "Have you spoken to your mother lately?"

Caleb's brows rose. "This is about my mother?"

"I think you may want to ask her that." Palmer bounced the ball in Caleb's direction and he caught it. "And that's all I'm going to say on the matter."

His friend shot the ball at him rather than the basket. "You know, don't you? You know who she's seeing."

Palmer grimaced. "Come on. I need a shower."

Oh, he had no intention of telling his friend directly about his mother and Philippidis. But he knew that it wouldn't take long for him to figure it out.

And that was okay. Because Philippidis was a rat bastard. And he didn't deserve a woman of Phoebe's caliber. Besides, he didn't want to see her get hurt. Well, at least any more than she had to. Because he had the feeling that lunch hadn't represented their first date.

At any rate, he had a list of problems of his own that he had to face. And face them, he would. Right after this shower and a good night's rest he hoped would bring him clarity and direction.

THE FOLLOWING MORNING didn't go as Palmer anticipated, with loose endings unraveling from his neatly rolled endeavors and demanding to be dealt with. The day was long, and he was tired when he finally rolled back into Earnest just before sunset. He thought about checking into the bed-and-breakfast again before doing anything else, then eyed the storm clouds gathering in the western sky.

Finally, it appeared it was going to rain.

He drew the car to a stop outside his father's house and killed the engine, his gaze drawn to the house in which he'd grown up. Lights flickered inside, indicating that his father had likely taken his dinner in front of the television again. Grasping a bag of groceries he'd picked up just outside town, he got out of the car and stepped up the walkway. To his relief, the front door was open and the screen door was unlocked.

He rapped on the outside then walked inside.

"Evening, Pops," he said.

His father nearly fell out of his chair, tipping the TV tray on its side, sending a glass of milk arcing across the room.

It seemed his father hadn't left the door open by way of welcome; he'd thought he wasn't coming back....

THE PHONE PRACTICALLY RANG off the hook with the news that Palmer was back in town.

Penelope cleaned up the table after dinner, purposely taking her time loading the dishwasher and wiping down the counters as she listened to her grandmother and aunt alternately field calls that were motivated purely by gossip, no matter how much Agatha tried to argue differently.

But despite her irritation at the intrusion, it felt like a swarm of fireflies lit her from the inside out, fluttering around her stomach and filling her with anticipation.

He was back.

She ignored the voice that asked, "how long, this time?" and instead focused on what she needed to do now that she had no excuse not to talk to him.

"Daisy says he stopped at his father's first," her aunt shared, coming in to replenish her glass of lemonade as she took a break from the telephone. "But I don't think things went well."

"How can you be sure?" Penelope folded and refolded the kitchen towel on the counter.

"Because a neighbor reports that there was a lot of shouting and sounds of stuff breaking."

Penelope raised her brows. "Stuff?"

"Well, obviously, it had to be glass or something, or she wouldn't have heard it." Her aunt stopped for a moment. "Or it could have been wood. But why would anyone want to break wood?"

"Why would anyone want to break anything at all?"

"Good point."

Her grandmother came in. "I shut off the ringer so we can have a few minutes' peace," she said with a long sigh.

"What's the latest?"

"He just checked back into Foss's."

The two older women turned to look at Penelope.

"What?"

Surely, they didn't expect her to go traipsing over there at this time of night?

Yes, she realized, they did.

She crossed her arms over her chest. "It's waited this long, it can hold till morning."

"Or until he leaves again?"

The bottom of her stomach dropped out at the easily said words. As though it wasn't a matter of "if" he would leave again, but "when."

"If he's checked in, he's not going anywhere until morning," she asserted.

"Maybe," her great-aunt said.

"Maybe not," her grandmother followed up.

"Oh, for Pete's sake, stop it already. I am not going over there."

Even the dog seemed to be staring at her expectantly as he sat at her feet.

"Why not?" her grandmother wanted to know.

Penelope waggled a finger at her. "You...I..." She heaved a sigh. "Don't start, okay?"

"I wasn't aware that I'd stopped."

Thor barked and then went to the door and came back again.

"It's the heat," her aunt said. "It's getting to all of us, I think."

She began to leave the room.

"Don't turn on the air conditioner," her grandmother called after her.

"Who's turning on the air? I'm plugging the phone back in. Given how stubborn the two of you are, nothing more's going to happen in there."

Penelope stared at her grandmother as if to say, "See?"

"That doesn't make you right," she said.

"It doesn't make you right either," Penelope countered, aware of the ridiculousness of their tit-for-tat but unable to stop herself.

Thor ran back and forth to the door again.

"I'm going to sit out back with the dog," she said.

Her grandmother stepped in the direction of the door.

Penelope held up her hand. "Alone. I'm going out there to sit alone."

"I thought you might want some company."

"I've had about all the company I can handle for one day, thank you very much."

She turned, nearly tripping over Thor. She pushed open the screen door with a screech of springs, waiting until he bounded out before following him.

Penelope closed her eyes and took a deep breath of the heavy air. It smelled like rain.

The dog was off like a shot, making a beeline for the gazebo. She squinted in that direction, wishing it were lighter so she could see better. She ended up seeing well enough as she made out a familiar shape outside.

Palmer...

19

PALMER HAD HOPED THAT Penelope would come outside. And he knew a moment of profound relief when she stepped through the back door and onto the porch. The kitchen light illuminated her from behind, turning her light, summery dress almost translucent and spotlighting her soft, sexy curves.

The thought of staying in his room at the B and B alone after what had gone down at his father's was too much to bear. He was wound up, needed to talk to someone.

And that someone was Penelope.

"Hey, boy," he said to the dog as he crouched down to scratch his ears.

Penelope came to stand before him, her arms crossed in front of her as if she was in need of warming, although the temperature was still sweltering.

He rose to his feet. "Hi."

He heard her swallow. "Hi."

Silence. And not of the comfortable variety either.

He reminded himself that circumstances hadn't been exactly ideal the last time they were together. The scene at Makeout Cove could have come straight out of an Owen Wilson movie.

"Is everything…okay?" he asked.

She blinked several times. "Okay? Define okay."

"With the sheriff."

Her face registered surprise. "Oh. Yes, um, he and I agreed that it's better for everyone involved if we parted ways." She looked over her shoulder toward the house. "Not that we were ever truly a couple. We dated awhile, but…"

She looked back at him and scrunched up her face.

"What are you doing here, Palmer?"

It was his turn to look surprised. "I'm not sure I understand the question."

She paced a short ways away and then came back. "I thought you were gone."

Funny, his father had believed the same thing. "I had to go to Seattle for a few days."

She nodded, but he wondered if she truly understood. "I heard the project was closed down."

"Yes."

She refused to meet his gaze.

"Is this what this is all about? You thought since the site was closed down that I had left again?"

She stared at him. "What? I should have believed differently?"

"I wouldn't leave without saying goodbye, Penelope."

"How am I supposed to know that?"

Restless energy filled him. He walked around her and then turned toward her again. "Because you know me."

"Do I? I thought I did once. But no longer."

"And what's changed between now and then?"

She searched his face and then looked away, appearing to bite her bottom lip.

Then her eyes widened. "My God, what happened?"

She neared him, lifting her hand to his right brow. She pressed her fingertips there and then looked at the bit of blood that covered them.

Palmer grimaced. "My father's way of welcoming me back."

A sound came from the direction of the house. They both looked to find the curtains on the back window fluttering. Penelope took his hand and led him inside the gazebo. He blinked when she turned on an overhead light.

"When did you guys put that in?"

"A couple years ago. Grandma was dating an electrician and she took full advantage. Hold still."

He hadn't realized that he'd flinched away from her touch.

"You need stitches."

"I need to have my head examined."

"Literally."

He stepped beyond her reach. "I'm fine."

"I'm serious, Palmer. You really should have that looked at."

"I said I'm fine."

They stood staring at each other for long moments. Then, finally, she flicked the switch again, sending them back into darkness.

His eyes adjusted to the light change as he sat down on the cushioned bench and she did the same opposite him, much as they'd done that first night.

"Tell me," she whispered.

His chest was tight. "Tell you what?"

"Tell me what happened."

He shrugged and clasped his hands between his knees. "Not much to tell, really. I came back into town, stopped by my father's to drop off some groceries and see how he was doing…" He gestured to his cut brow. "And this is what I got by way of thanks."

"He hit you?"

He grimaced. "He tried to. I ducked the blow and he shoved me toward the door instead. I lost my footing and tripped over the meal he'd been eating and hit my head on the jamb."

"Neighbors said they heard things breaking."

Great. By now the entire town of Earnest knew what had gone down at his father's.

"Palmer?"

He sat back and drew a deep breath. "Yeah. His, um, TV tray holding his dinner tipped over…"

"On its own?"

"No. He was so shocked to see me walk in, he knocked it over."

She reached across to touch his knee. He trapped her hand under his.

She cleared her throat. "You know, there were a lot of those…accidents when we were in high school…"

Palmer didn't dare say a word.

"Oh, you could pawn some of them off on football practice or tussling with the guys…but…" She tightened her grip on his knee. "But you can't live in a town this small without someone knowing the truth."

No one had ever breathed a word of it to Palmer. He'd thought he was suffering his own private hell behind the closed doors of the DeVoe house.

"My grandmother says that a couple of people tried to step in. The pastor. A neighbor. But your father wouldn't listen to reason."

"Christ," Palmer said under his breath.

"I'm…sorry," she whispered. "I didn't know until later, after you'd left. Had I…"

"What would you have done?"

"There had to be some sort of mechanism in place. Someone to be contacted."

"There was. The sheriff. But aside from warning my father, there was little else he could do."

Penelope fell silent.

"It's funny, but growing up, things were pretty normal. It wasn't until I was in high school that it escalated.

My mother…my mother tried to stop him. But once she died…"

She gasped.

"I thought that now…when I came back…that maybe, finally, things could be different."

He shook his head, remembering the scene at the house earlier.

"I can't believe that even at his age, he wanted to hit me. He nearly did more damage to himself than me."

"Palmer!" She took both his hands in hers, holding them tightly.

"I don't know, Penelope. I don't know if I can handle it. Not now. Tonight I nearly raised my hand to him…"

She didn't say anything for a long moment. "But you didn't."

"No. No, I didn't."

Her shoulders seemed to droop in relief.

"But the mere fact that I wanted to hit him…however briefly…it scared the hell out of me."

"I can understand that."

He turned his hands in hers, running the pads of his fingers over knuckles and smooth nails. "Can you? Because I can't."

"Maybe he…"

He waited. "Don't make excuses for him, Penelope. My mother used to do it. I couldn't bear that."

"No. No excuses." She drew in a deep breath. "Do you know what set him off?"

He thought about it now. He hadn't considered it at the time. Then he looked up into her shadowy face. "He'd thought I left."

"He's not the only one…"

PENELOPE'S CHEST FELT LIKE it might collapse in on itself. She hurt for Palmer in a way that manifested itself as an almost physical pain. As if she had momentarily experienced every blow he had suffered as a child.

She'd been heartbroken when she'd learned what he'd suffered through. He'd been gone a full two years before her grandmother had mentioned something about Palmer's father's temper. He'd gotten into an argument of some sort with the gas station attendant and had been arrested for assault.

It was then that her grandmother had shared what it seemed everyone but she had known.

She couldn't imagine not having anyone else in the world. Oh, her mother might be flighty, but her grandmother and great-aunt had always been there.

Palmer on the other hand…

"After your mother died, you really didn't have anyone, did you?" she whispered.

He coughed quietly. "I had you."

Palmer's hair was tousled as if he'd run his hands through it; his shirt was wrinkled; his face looked drawn as if he hadn't gotten a good night's sleep for perhaps longer than she had.

But that wasn't possible. Because she had fifteen years of sleepless nights on him.

A small voice supplied a litany of reasons why she shouldn't tell him her news now. Shouldn't reveal the secret she'd kept for so very long. He looked as if he'd been to hell already; she didn't have it in her to send him back there so quickly.

"Penelope." Her name exited his mouth like a melodious note.

Her stomach tightened and need instantly pooled in her lower belly, providing her with even more reasons to delay the inevitable…

Instead, she slid her hand slowly from his. "I have something to tell you, Palmer…" Penelope didn't have a choice. If she didn't tell him now, she was afraid she might never do it.

Spit it out. Before you lose your nerve again and give in to the desire to kiss him.

"You might want to brace yourself for this…"

"This is that thing from the pub, isn't it?" he asked. "The thing you had to tell me and didn't."

She looked down into her lap and nodded.

"And you want to tell me now."

The statement was almost accusatory. She met his gaze. "I'm sorry that it has to come now…like this. But I…well, your father wasn't the only one who'd thought you'd left again. I…I did, too."

Everyone had. The buzz was all over town that

he'd driven straight out of town the same way he had before.

"I've tried to tell you a thousand different ways. Wished I could have told you sooner." The weight of her admission weighed against her chest like a cannonball. "I've come to the conclusion that there is no right place, right way to say what I have to, Palmer. I'm sorry if it's the last thing you want to hear. I have to say it. I've kept it to myself for far too long." Her throat tried to refuse her a breath. "You deserve to know."

Her words seemed to ring through the gazebo and then drop like bricks on the wood floor between them.

"Penelope…"

"No, please. Don't. I'm going to say it. Just give me a second."

Outside, she heard Thor panting. The sound of clinking silverware. A train horn from out on the other side of Old Man Benson's cornfields.

And her heart thundered so loud it nearly deafened her.

"Palmer, I…when you left fifteen years ago…"

Damnit, just say the words!

He shifted uncomfortably. "This goes back fifteen years?"

She nodded. "Yes. Yes, it does. You see, when you shared the news that you were leaving back then, everything was fine. I knew it was something you had to do. You'd dreamed about heading off on your own and making a name for yourself...."

"I asked you to come."

She laughed without humor. "I know. And I thought about it. Really, I did. I would have liked nothing better than to have packed everything and run away with you..."

"But...?"

"But...I couldn't. Three months before you were to go I...found out I was pregnant."

His quick intake of breath stole every sound from the air around them.

There. She had said it. Finally. She'd told him.

And she felt worse than she'd thought she might. Far worse. As if her very skin had been stripped from her body and there was nowhere for her to hide.

"I don't understand," he said so quietly she nearly didn't hear him. "Are you saying you were pregnant... with my...with our child?"

She nodded and looked down to find her hands clenched so tightly in her lap they'd lost feeling.

"And you didn't tell me?"

She shook her head. "I...I couldn't. You were so excited. You had all your plans laid carefully out." Her voice caught. "Every day you outlined what you were going to do, where you were going to go and how you would get there..."

Silence.

It seemed to drag out forever as she waited for his response.

"What happened to the baby?"

There it was. The question she had dreaded. The question that rang in her ears for the past fifteen years.

"He...our son...your son...was born on March 15th... and I gave him up for adoption."

20

"I'M SORRY...SO VERY SORRY..." Penelope's words sliced into his ear like needles he couldn't remove. "I didn't know what to do. You were so happy. So hopeful. Pursuing a dream you'd spent your whole life planning. I just couldn't ruin it for you..."

He saw the tears rolling down Penelope's face, how they glistened in the dim light, but he was too shocked to comfort her. He was too busy trying to find a way to swallow the secret she was sharing with him. A secret she'd kept from him for fifteen years.

"My grandmother...my aunt... They helped me. I stayed with friends in Seattle when I started showing. The story was I had a summer internship, so nobody knew, although I'm sure a few guessed..."

Palmer grabbed her arms as if to stop her from leaving, but she hadn't made a move to go anywhere. "Stop! Don't say another word. Please...just be quiet for a moment."

It didn't make any sense. None of it.

How was it possible that he had a child out there, a son, and hadn't known about him? How could Penelope have done what she had without telling him?

Surprise, grief, betrayal slashed through him like a knife, threatening what was already a tenuous hold he had on the current reality of his life.

He didn't want to hear this. Didn't want to know. Why was she telling him this? Why was she saying this now?

He had a fourteen-year-old son out there…somewhere…

He finally focused on Penelope's pale face, noting the fear there. Hating that he had inspired it. On the heels of what he'd shared about his father, he could only imagine what was going through her mind.

And she might have been right. Because in that one moment Palmer felt an urge greater than any he'd ever experienced to lash out at something physically. To release the roiling emotions that nearly overwhelmed him.

He released her instead.

She sat back.

He got up.

"Palmer, please," she pled.

"I…I have to go…"

"I need for you to understand…"

But it was too much for him to take in all at once.

He needed time. Space to think. The chance to absorb all that was said.

And an urgent need to leave Earnest, Washington, all over again. This time for good.

PALMER WASN'T PAYING ATTENTION to how fast he was going. He just drove down the darkened highway, his hands so tight on the wheel, his knuckles appeared about to emerge through his skin. He shouldn't have been surprised when he heard the burst of a siren and spotted the flashing lights behind him.

He hit the steering wheel with his palm. Damn. Damn, damn, damn.

He considered outrunning the sheriff who no doubt had revenge on his mind. Experience told him that he wouldn't chase him outside county lines.

Instead, he forced his foot off the gas pedal and coasted to a stop on the right side of the road, flicking on his hazard lights.

It seemed to take forever for the sheriff to get out of his car. Despite the darkness, he wore mirrored sunglasses and had put on his hat. He looked like a Hollywood movie cliché as he sauntered up to the driver's side window and shined a bright flashlight inside, blinding Palmer as he checked out the interior of the car.

Palmer offered up his license and registration on the leased Mercedes.

"Do you know how fast you were going?" Barnaby asked.

"No, sir. I'm sorry, I wasn't paying attention."

The sheriff looked over the document in his hand. "You don't own the vehicle."

"No, sir."

In fact, it had emerged that he had nothing of a permanent nature in Earnest. Everything was leased or borrowed.

Or had been stolen away.

It would be all too easy to just accept the ticket he knew he was about to get and just keep moving. Drive up to Seattle, to the airport, not stopping until he was safely in the Northeast, back to the life he had forged for himself, the life he knew.

"Where you going?" Barnaby asked.

"Seattle."

He nodded and handed the documents back to him. "Watch your speed from here on out."

Palmer squinted at him, watching as he switched off his flashlight and turned back toward his car.

"You're not going to issue me a ticket?"

Barnaby stopped. "Why? Do you want one?"

For reasons he couldn't pin down, he felt like he deserved one. "No."

"Then I'm letting you go with a warning." He continued walking back toward his car.

"Barnaby?"

"If you don't leave in the next five seconds, DeVoe, I am going to issue you that ticket."

"I just wanted to say thank you," he said. "And to ask you to look out after Penelope."

The sheriff froze, flashlight tapping against the side of his leg. "That's no longer my job, DeVoe. It's yours."

He got into his car, shut off his blinking lights, and drove around Palmer as he sat at the side of the road.

"RISE AND SHINE, SLEEPYHEAD. The sun is smiling."

"Tell it to go away." Penelope burrowed further down under the covers. She didn't want to get up. She just wanted to lie in bed until the world started spinning correctly on its axis again. When she could accurately interpret how Palmer had taken the news. When she could stop feeling so guilty her skin felt sticky with it.

"It's been two days. Don't you think it's long past time you sucked it up and got on with your life again?" her grandmother asked. "Your aunt and I can't make heads or tails out of your shipping system at the shop. And, frankly, we're getting a little tired of opening for you."

"So don't. I didn't ask you to."

She felt her mattress shift and guessed Agatha had sat down on it. "Well, at least you're speaking. That's a start. I might not like what you're saying, but that's nothing new."

Penelope squeezed her eyes shut, wishing her away.

"You didn't think it would be easy, did you?"

The words penetrated the covers and invaded her

ears. She blinked her eyes open, remembering Palmer's look of anguish when she'd told him they had a son.

Raw pain washed over her anew, and she felt like throwing up.

"How did you know I told him?" she whispered.

"Surely you jest, child. Haven't you figured out that I know everything by now?"

She lay still.

"Okay, I saw you two in the gazebo. And then you dove straight for your bed from which you've yet to emerge. So that means either you're boycotting the increasing price of postage stamps, or you finally told the man he's a father."

Penelope bit hard on her bottom lip.

Her grandmother smacked her hip. "I'm going to go make some of my world famous French toast. If you want a piece, I suggest you get up and take a shower first. You stink."

The weight lifted from the bed and then she heard her door close. Penelope didn't trust that her grandmother was not still in the room so she didn't move for a long moment, listening for sounds. The ones she heard came from the direction of the kitchen.

She rolled over to her back and pulled the covers down with a jerk but didn't get up. Instead, she stared intently at the ceiling that was in dire need of a coat of paint…and that she prayed would somehow offer up the answers she was seeking.

So caught up had she been in summoning up the

courage to tell Palmer her secret, she had been woefully unprepared for what his reaction might be. How stupid of her. How dumb she'd been not to be ready to offer him some sort of reassurance. Done something, anything, to stop him from leaving her alone in the gazebo.

Stop him from leaving Earnest.

She recalled yesterday morning's visit from Barnaby. Oh, she hadn't spoken to him. Instead, she'd listened as her grandmother and aunt fussed over him in the living room, offering him coffee, breakfast or whatever his li'l heart desired if he'd just stick around until Penelope got up.

But Penelope had had no intention of getting up. Especially not since she'd heard Barnaby say that he'd pulled Palmer over on his way out of town the night before…and that he'd asked Barnaby to look after her.

The sheriff, apparently, had feared there was something wrong, thus the reason for his visit.

There was something wrong, Penelope thought now. But it wasn't something a sheriff, a grandmother or a great-aunt could fix. And this particular repair also appeared to lie outside her own range of expertise.

The sweet scent of cinnamon teased her nostrils. She groaned and pulled the covers back up. But there were a few things a mortal being wasn't capable of resisting. And her grandmother's French toast was one of them…

PALMER HAD SAT AT THE SIDE of the road for an hour, his hazards blinking, absently watching the moon rise, willing the pain inside him away.

How easy it would be to leave. To just keep on going. To put behind him that chaos.

He'd come back to Earnest with so much hope for the future. Hope that had grown when Penelope had welcomed him back, and his father had briefly accepted his presence in his house.

How had it all turned so completely, utterly bad?

He'd started the car back up, and heedless of Barnaby's warning, had flattened the gas pedal, heading in the same direction he had been, watching Earnest's few lights get dimmer and dimmer in his rearview mirror.

Then he'd experienced something he hadn't expected. Something that had caused him to stand on the brakes, stopping in the middle of the road after the car had skidded.

He'd known a sick sense of what it must have been like for Penelope all those years ago.

Pregnant.

Alone.

The father of her child on his way out of town to follow a dream of wealth and success.

How could he have been so blind? How could he have missed the signs? With the hindsight of twenty-twenty vision, he'd recalled the way her demeanor had changed in the months before his departure. How she had appeared more wan and seemed sick a lot of the time. He'd been so consumed with his own plans, he hadn't stopped to take a good look at her. Had taken at face value her reassurances that she couldn't possibly come with him, and that she was only missing him already.

Stupid, stupid, stupid.

Then there was the boy...

"It was the only thing I could think to do," she'd told him in the gazebo before he'd shut her down. "I was only eighteen, with two crazy old women in my life. What was I going to do with a baby who deserved two loving parents? A family in a position to offer him everything neither of us had had? A family that couldn't have children of their own and who would love him even more because he was a child they had chosen..."

A horn had honked as a pickup had come up behind him and then tentatively passed him before continuing on.

"There are days when I regret my decision," she'd whispered. "And there isn't a second that goes by that I don't feel his presence out there somewhere. That I don't love him and wonder what he's doing at that exact moment..."

She'd gone on to explain how she'd registered her name and contact information with various agencies to make it easier for their son in case he wanted to find her. It was the main reason she'd purchased computer equipment and hooked her business up to the internet. While the café was slow, she checked the pages she'd posted on adoption sites and bulletin boards stating the name of their son, his birthday, along with a message of love and an invitation to seek her out.

So far there had been no word, she'd said. But she knew that one day he would want to know the truth. And she wanted to be there to give it to him.

"And me?" Palmer had asked, his ears still ringing with her admission. "What had you planned to tell him about me?"

She'd looked down. "I don't know. I figured I'd know what to do when the time came..."

She'd blinked up at him. "I suppose that decision is now up to you."

Palmer's mind had gone blank then, as dark as the two-lane highway that stretched outside his windshield.

Without being aware that he'd made the decision, he'd put the car in gear, turning back toward Earnest.

Come what may, he had to see this through.

And he had to tell Penelope how sorry he was for having left her all those years before.

21

"HE'S BOUGHT THE OLD Olyphant house."

Penelope fumbled the gravy boat she was placing on the kitchen table while her aunt stuck her fingers into the bowl of mashed potatoes. The words had come from her grandmother who had just gotten off the phone.

"What?" Irene asked.

"Palmer DeVoe. Twila just phoned to say that he bought the old Olyphant place across from his father's house. Paid a pretty penny for it, too. The agent—you know, Jolie, the oldest Frazer girl—said she purposely inflated the price, expecting him to counter. Instead he just wrote out a check for the amount in full. On the spot."

Penelope tipped over the gravy boat.

It was a full week since she and Palmer had spoken in the gazebo. A full seven days during which she'd moved from despair to functional automaton to a semblance of normalcy, working with hope toward the day when she wouldn't spend every waking moment thinking about the expression he'd worn when she'd revealed her secret.

"I don't understand," Irene said, as if voicing her own thoughts. "I thought he left town? Surely, if he was back, we'd have heard from Debra Foss at the B and B."

"He's not staying at the bed-and-breakfast," Agatha said.

"Then where is he staying?"

Penelope swallowed hard at her grandmother's answer. "His father's."

But since when? After Barnaby's visit, everyone had believed Palmer had left again. And Penelope had been sure that this time it was for good. Considering everything he'd been through on that fateful day—coming to terms with the possibility that his relationship with his father might not be salvageable, and then being told that he had a fourteen-year-old son out there somewhere being raised by an unknown family he had no way of contacting—she'd expected him to go back to the east coast and never look back.

But he was here…

And he hadn't been in contact with her…

She wasn't sure which hurt the most. That he was nearby…or that he was nearby and hadn't been by to see her.

Both, she decided.

Before, she'd functioned knowing he was far away, out of her immediate orbit, beyond her touch.

Knowing he was here in town and wasn't a part of her life, hurt as much as when she handed their son over to the nurse for the final time.

"Penelope?" her grandmother said.

She blinked, realizing the gravy was spilling into a puddle on the white tablecloth and dripping over the side of the table near her feet.

"I'm not hungry," she said, hurrying from the room.

She heard Irene say, "What fool thing were you thinking telling her that? Now she's going to dive back under those covers. Lord knows when we'll see her again."

"Better she should find out sooner than later," her grandmother countered.

Better Palmer should have left town as they all thought he'd had, Penelope thought as she closed her bedroom door. She slowly slid down the smooth wood to sit on the floor, the walls of her chest threatening to collapse and crush everything inside...

"NOT BAD," CALEB SAID as he and Palmer finished a walk-through of the Olyphant property. "She needs a lot of work, but she has great bones."

Palmer didn't tell his friend that he'd bought the place without having stepped a foot inside. For all he knew, it could have been stripped down to the copper piping.

Caleb leaned against the open doorway, staring out at the overgrown back lawn. The grass was cut, but shrubs and roses had run wild, taking over the edges of the yard.

"So...you're here to stay then," his friend said quietly.

Palmer drew in a deep breath. "I could be looking to flip the place."

Caleb glanced over his shoulder at him. "Uh huh. In this booming real estate market."

He grinned. "I could always sell the place to you when you marry Bryna Metaxas."

His friend coughed so hard, Palmer thumped him on the back to help him through the fit.

"I'm sorry. Did I say something I shouldn't?"

"Yes, you did, indeed." Caleb's comical grimace was back. "Considering that her brothers still consider me as suitable as a member of al-Qaeda, well, I don't see that happening anytime soon." He looked down at his expensive leather loafers. "Anyway, Bryna doesn't seem to be in any hurry."

"Oh?"

Caleb pushed off the doorjamb and came to stand in front of him. "I didn't come over here to talk about my love life," he said. "I'm here to talk about yours."

Palmer stepped around him back down the hall and into the living room, his friend following on his heels. "That's a topic that's not up for discussion."

"Oh?" he mimicked.

"I have enough going on right now without adding that to the list."

And it was the truth, wasn't it? While he was essentially living with his father, having forced himself on the old man, the atmosphere between them was tense at best, contentious at worst. But every time he thought about leaving, he went into the bedroom where his mother had slept alone in the last months of her life, and which his father had left untouched, and reminded himself how much she had wanted them to work things out. How she'd wanted them to come together rather than drift apart.

And tried not to think about how much she would have loved being a grandmother.

Then he'd think about stopping on that deserted highway, caught at a crossroads. There was no going forward for him. Not anymore. Not without resolving what he'd left behind first.

Caleb said, "So word has it Philippidis is going to sue you for breach."

"I knew it was a possibility."

"Try certainty."

"Yes, well, just wait until the competition clause comes into play."

"How do you mean? You're thinking about going ahead with your plans alone?"

Palmer shook his head. "I have resources, but not quite enough to go head-to-head with Philippidis."

"Who does?"

He considered his friend. "Do you want to go for a ride?"

Caleb looked around. "Lead on."

The house wasn't the only investment Palmer had made. He'd turned in his leased car and bought an SUV hybrid. Caleb made appreciative sounds as he drove toward the destination he had in mind.

"So," he said carefully. "Have you had that talk with your mother yet?"

Caleb's expression darkened.

"I'll take that as a no."

"A partial no."

Palmer glanced at him.

"I called her and she sensed immediately what was up."

"And?"

"And she hung up on me."

Palmer raised his brows.

"After she told me to thank you for your discretion."

He grimaced. "Guilty as charged."

"I would have killed you had I found out later and discovered you'd known."

"Ah, but my reasons were more self-serving than that."

"I suspected."

Palmer pulled into the gravel road leading to the old work site. The trailer had a padlock on it, but otherwise everything was the same. Including the fact that no one was there.

"This the place?" Caleb asked as they got out of the car.

"Yep."

His friend palmed the padlock. "Works fast, doesn't he?"

"I expected nothing different." Palmer led the way toward the equipment nearer the construction site. He wasn't disappointed to find the keys in many of the machines. He climbed into the cab of a bulldozer and started up the engine.

"What are you going to do?" Caleb shouted over the cacophony.

"Watch and learn," he called back. "And in case you're interested, the keys are in the loader over there..."

"Palmer DeVoe completely destroyed his work site this morning along with that guy that's been spotted around town with the Metaxas girl."

Penelope eyed her aunt over her soup. She released her grip on her spoon and grimaced when it disappeared into the depths of her bowl. "I have a request."

"Oh?" her grandmother said.

She fished her spoon out and cleaned the handle with her napkin. "If a sentence begins, ends with or contains anywhere in between the name Palmer DeVoe, I don't want to hear it."

Agatha shrugged. "Then plug your ears. Because when it comes to gossip right now, that name is the only game in town."

Game.

Penelope stretched the kinks out of her neck and took

another bite of minestrone. It was too damn hot to be eating soup, but try explaining that to Agatha and Irene, who had gotten tired of eating sandwiches and potato salad and every other cold dish over the past month because of the heat wave.

They never did get that rain the weatherman had forecast. But surely it couldn't possibly keep up like this. At some point they would return to their regularly scheduled doom and gloom with rain nearly every day.

Penelope knew the heat was only partly responsible for her mood. She hadn't gotten much sleep in the past few days and it was beginning to take its toll on her. She was short tempered and slow moving.

"So...you haven't heard from him yet?" her grandmother asked.

"Yet? What makes you think I will?"

Agatha shrugged again. "Call it women's intuition."

Aunt Irene laughed. "That and the tarot cards."

Penelope gave an eye roll.

"His staying in town...it's got to be a good sign, right?" Irene asked after her sister elbowed her.

"A good sign of what?"

"For you two."

Penelope gave up on the soup. "There is no us two."

She got up and dumped the contents of her bowl into the sink.

Her grandmother sighed. "Fix yourself a sandwich. You look like we're denying you food."

She was right. Of course. She sat down to eat with them every day, but ended up eating very little of whatever was on offer. Partly because they kept bringing up Palmer. Mostly because her stomach didn't like what she was trying to feed it.

She needed to see Palmer. If only to fill him in on her efforts to find their…his son. And to ask if he'd like to be added to the contact information.

It was fine if he didn't want to see her any more than he had to. She couldn't blame him for that. But their son…well, she'd like it if his father was as receptive as she was to the possibility of meeting him.

She leaned against the counter, absently chewing a bite of a ham sandwich. She placed the other half next to her aunt's soup bowl and then headed for the door.

"Where are you going?" her grandmother called after her.

"Back to work. Where else would I be going?"

Where else, indeed?

22

"DAMN! I HAVEN'T FELT this great in a long, damn time," Caleb proclaimed a couple of hours later after the two had lunch at the Quality Diner.

Palmer chuckled. "I think Bryna might be interested in hearing that."

Caleb's grin was full. "She's not worried."

Palmer had met Bryna on a couple of occasions. At first, he'd been surprised that she'd been younger than Caleb. But while his friend held the chronological advantage, Bryna trumped him in every other way, throwing him off balance and, yes, making Caleb Payne a little more easygoing.

Or, at the very least, happier.

"So what's on tap next?" Caleb asked when they'd climbed back into his car.

"What? This morning wasn't enough?"

His friend looked at him. "If I know you—and I do—you have something else up your sleeve."

As it stood, he did have one last ace to play. One he'd been holding on to. And now was as good a time as any to play it.

"Unless it doesn't include me..." Caleb ventured.

"Pardon?"

"You know, plans of a personal nature?"

Palmer's mind went immediately to Penelope and he experienced the all too familiar tightening of his groin, although now it was combined with a tight ball of emotion in his solar plexus.

"No. This, I think you'll enjoy almost as much as what we did before lunch."

Ten minutes later, Palmer pulled his car into the lot of the old Metaxas lumber mill. He felt Caleb's questioning gaze on him, but didn't respond as he parked and climbed out.

"What are we doing here? I'm not sure I'm welcome. Actually, I'm positive I'm unwelcome."

"Bear with me," Palmer said, leading the way inside.

He didn't stop until he stood outside the main offices. Through a glass wall, he spotted Troy Metaxas talking on the phone.

"Gary, I'm going to have to call you back," Troy's voice reached them. "Yes, yes. I know. Five minutes."

He hung up the phone and came around the desk, clearly surprised and wary of his two guests.

"Palmer," he said, extending his hand. "Caleb."

Palmer noticed that he didn't offer to shake Caleb's hand and was amused.

He also noticed that Bryna had come out of what must be her office and stood behind them with Troy's younger brother Ari.

"Can I talk to you a minute?" Palmer asked.

Troy's gaze trailed to his sister and then Caleb. "May I ask what this is concerning? Shall I call my attorneys?"

"Or the sheriff," Caleb muttered under his breath.

Palmer cleared his throat. "Invite us into your office and you'll find out…"

PENELOPE WAS READY to jump out of her skin. If Palmer was hoping to punish her for her crimes, he couldn't have chosen a more effective weapon. His silence was wearing on her like sandpaper, rubbing her raw emotionally.

She lay in bed staring at the dappled moonlight against the far wall. She wished it would rain, already. The heat only made it doubly difficult to find a swath of peace from which she could cut an hour or two of much-needed sleep.

She sighed and sat upright, giving up. The clock told her it was after midnight. Surely, even her grandmother and great-aunt should be asleep by now.

She got up and got dressed, deciding a walk might do her a bit of good. Thankfully Earnest was safe enough to do that late at night.

She quietly opened her bedroom door a crack and peeked out. The flicker of candlelight came from the direction of the kitchen.

Damn.

Damn, damn, damn, damn.

She didn't think she could handle another tarot session with Agatha and Irene.

She closed the door again and considered her options. It would be the second time she'd snuck out of her bedroom window in a few weeks. But what other choice did she have?

She opened the window and eyed the bushes. To avoid them, she had to launch herself just right...

She landed smack dab in the middle. And heard Thor's bark from somewhere inside the house.

Struggling to a standing position, she straightened her dress and hurried out toward the street.

She was so intent on getting out of there, she didn't acknowledge the two faces in the front window watching after her. Or respond when her grandmother said to her great-aunt, "See. I told you."

PALMER KNOCKED OUT a section of drywall in the kitchen of the old Olyphant place and stood back to let the dust settle. He pulled down his paper facemask and considered his handiwork. After eating dinner with his father, and watching television with him, mostly in silence, he'd waited until the old man had gone to bed and then headed across the street to start working on the place.

He'd decided to begin with the kitchen first, since that was one of the most important rooms. Thankfully, it wouldn't need much major work, other than tile and countertops, after he finished replacing this section of drywall that looked like someone had either put his hand through or fallen against...hard.

He brushed the dust off the sleeve of his T-shirt and then rubbed the sweat off his brow with it, reliving the scene at the mill even as he worked.

"I don't understand," Troy Metaxas had said once he'd outlined his proposal.

Next to him, Caleb had finally gotten it and chuckled quietly while he rubbed his chin.

"I'm saying that I'm throwing in with you, if you'll have me," Palmer had said.

And, as he'd hoped but hadn't dared to expect, Caleb had said the same.

"Separate, we may not be strong enough to beat Philippidis at his own game," Palmer had gone on. "But together, and with Caleb and my unique view from the other side of the field...well, we just might be able to do this."

And so was born a handshake deal that would probably bring on a whole lot of legal hurt from Philippidis's lawyers. But, damn, he was tired of playing by rules others had made and never consulted him on.

Movement caught his attention. He turned around

quickly, not expecting to see anyone this late—or rather this early in the morning, outside his back door.

"Hi," Penelope said, looking like temptation incarnate…

PENELOPE HAD WALKED for nearly an hour before finding herself standing outside the old Olyphant house. She remembered the place well. When they'd all been younger, and Mr. Olyphant had shut himself inside with nothing but a fluttering curtain here and a missing newspaper there to indicate anyone was inside, the neighborhood kids liked to joke that he wasn't actually alive at all, but rather a ghost that inhabited the place.

Then they'd all pedal like the devil snapped at their heels to get away.

And now Palmer owned it.

She hadn't expected to see lights burning inside. Or hear the telltale thud that indicated someone was working at this late hour.

Before she knew it she was going around the back, surprised to find the rear door open.

And there stood Palmer, covered in sweat and drywall, wiping his brow against the sleeve of his T-shirt.

It wasn't fair that he should look so good. Despite his desk job, he had a body that could easily have handled a full day of the work he was now doing. Biceps bulged, jeans hugged his tight rear end, and his hair was nicely disheveled, begging fingers to tunnel into the thick, unruly depths.

She was so transfixed that she didn't immediately notice that he'd spotted her.

"Hi," she said lamely.

He didn't say anything for a long moment, then he pulled the mask hanging around his neck up over his head and put it on the debris-covered counter.

"Hi, yourself."

Penelope took a tentative step forward, looking around her as she did so. Everywhere but into his watchful, wary eyes.

"I couldn't sleep so I went for a walk and…well, before I knew it I was here." She cleared her throat. The kitchen was large and could easily accommodate both an island with stools and at least a six-chair table. "I'd heard you bought this place."

"Yes, word tends to get around fast here, doesn't it?"

She smiled. "I think everyone knew before the ink was even dry on the deed."

He nodded.

Penelope searched for the words she had planned to say once their paths finally crossed again…but now that she was here, she couldn't seem to summon a single one.

"Excuse me for a minute?" he said.

She blinked. "Sure."

She told herself she should leave. It wasn't a good idea to be alone with Palmer at any time, much less in the middle of the night. But she couldn't seem to transmit the idea to her feet.

So instead, she stood completely still, watching as he brushed dust from his T-shirt and went out into the hall and up the stairs. Moments later, she heard the squeak of an old faucet turn on.

Penelope considered the drywall he was repairing and then stepped farther into the room, staring down the hall to the airy foyer. It was a big, beautiful old place, with original woodwork and molding. It was the type of place that she once imagined they'd share together.

She jumped when he came back down the stairs.

Then she realized he'd taken a shower. Had he been gone that long? He must have, because his hair was damp and he wore a fresh pair of jeans and a clean T-shirt.

And he now looked as awkward as she felt.

Which couldn't be possible. Could it?

"I..." he began.

Penelope quickly held up her hand. "Wait. There are a few things I want to say first..."

It occurred to her that she'd nervously interrupted him and she rushed to apologize.

"I'm sorry. Go ahead. Say what you were going to say."

His gaze was steady on hers, his eyes unreadable. "That's okay. The floor is yours."

She looked down at that same floor and ordered her throat to loosen up. "I...I..."

She silently berated herself, trying to ignore the thick beating of her heart.

"I don't know. I guess I never expected you to come back to Earnest. And when you did, everything just happened so fast. There wasn't time for me to think. I had a hard time reconciling the past with the present..."

She cleared her throat.

"I never meant to hurt you, Palmer. It's important that you know that."

He appeared surprised. She cringed. This wasn't going at all the way she'd hoped.

She rushed on...and with every second that passed wished she had stayed a little farther back in those shadows.

She finally ran out of words and stood awkwardly, unable to meet his gaze for fear of what she might find there.

"Are you really apologizing to me?" he asked.

Her brows drew together.

"Because if you are, it's not accepted."

The emotion crowding her chest surged up into her throat. "I...understand..."

She began to turn to go. But his dropping to one knee in front of her stopped her cold.

"At least, not unless you also accept my apology."

She stood transfixed. "Palmer, I..."

"No, Penelope. You've had your say. Please allow me mine." He looked down and then back up. "This is not exactly the way I envisioned it, but I'm not going to let this opportunity pass like I've let so many others." He searched her eyes. "I should have done this fifteen years ago…"

It couldn't possibly be. None of it made sense to her. Her brain had stopped working about five minutes ago.

"I love you, Penelope. Always have. Always will. Nothing will ever change that." His expression darkened. "I can't begin to imagine what you went through so long ago. Or understand. All I can do is say I'm sorry you had to go through it alone…"

A stunned amazement suffused Penelope from her head to the tips of her toes.

"Marry me. Marry me now. Today. Tomorrow. Marry me."

She felt suddenly dizzy.

"Penelope?"

"I don't know what to say."

"Say yes. Say yes so we can continue a journey that should never have been sidetracked. Say yes so we can find our son and work on having others…or daughters, or both. Say yes so I can spend the rest of my life proving how much I love you…starting now."

"I never doubted your love," she whispered.

He got to his feet. "I know. And that makes you all the more special."

He crowded her to his chest, holding her tight.

"I don't know what to say."

He kissed her hair then murmured into her ear, "Say yes, Penelope."

"Yes." She said the word so softly she nearly didn't hear it herself. "Yes," she repeated, more loudly. "Yes!"

She put her hands on either side of his head and kissed him with unabashed love. Over and over and over again, drawing from a well of emotion so deep it would never run dry. Not in this life, or the next, or the one after that.

He swept her off her feet. Penelope gasped, holding tight as he turned toward the hall.

"Let me show you the rest of the house. I think you'll find the master bedroom of particular interest, wife-to-be, since it's the room we're going to be spending a great deal of time in…"

* * * * *

*See below for a sneak peek from our classic
Harlequin® Romance® line.*

Introducing DADDY BY CHRISTMAS by Patricia Thayer.

MIA caught sight of Jarrett when he walked into the open lobby. It was hard not to notice the man. In a charcoal business suit with a crisp white shirt and striped tie covered by a dark trench coat, he looked more Wall Street than small-town Colorado.

Mia couldn't blame him for keeping his distance. He was probably tired of taking care of her.

Besides, why would a man like Jarrett McKane be interested in her? Why would he want to take on a woman expecting a baby? Yet he'd done so many things for her. He'd been there when she'd needed him most. How could she not care about a man like that?

Heart pounding in her ears, she walked up behind him. Jarrett turned to face her. "Did you get enough sleep last night?"

"Yes, thanks to you," she said, wondering if he'd thought about their kiss. Her gaze went to his mouth, then she quickly glanced away. "And thank you for not bringing up my meltdown."

Jarrett couldn't stop looking at Mia. Blue was definitely her color, bringing out the richness of her eyes.

"What meltdown?" he said, trying hard to focus on what she was saying. "You were just exhausted from lack of sleep and worried about your baby."

He couldn't help remembering how, during the night, he'd kept going in to watch her sleep. How strange was that? "I hope you got enough rest."

She nodded. "Plenty. And you're a good neighbor for

coming to my rescue."

He tensed. Neighbor? *What neighbor kisses you like I did?* "That's me, just the full-service landlord," he said, trying to keep the sarcasm out of his voice. He started to leave, but she put her hand on his arm.

"Jarrett, what I meant was you went beyond helping me." Her eyes searched his face. "I've asked far too much of you."

"Did you hear me complain?"

She shook her head. "You should. I feel like I've taken advantage."

"Like I said, I haven't minded."

"And I'm grateful for everything…"

Grasping her hand on his arm, Jarrett leaned forward. The memory of last night's kiss had him aching for another. "I didn't do it for your gratitude, Mia."

Gorgeous tycoon Jarrett McKane has never believed in Christmas—but he can't help being drawn to soon-to-be-mom Mia Saunders! Christmases past were spent alone…and now Jarrett may just have a fairy-tale ending for all his Christmases future!

Available December 2010, only from Harlequin® Romance®.

HARLEQUIN®

A *Romance*

FOR EVERY MOOD™

Spotlight on
Classic

Quintessential, modern love stories
that are romance at its finest.

See the next page
to enjoy a sneak peek from
the Harlequin® Romance series.

HARLEQUIN *Presents*

Bestselling Harlequin Presents® author

Julia James

brings you her most powerful book yet…

FORBIDDEN OR FOR BEDDING?

The shamed mistress…

Guy de Rochemont's name is a byword for wealth
and power—and now his duty is to wed.

Alexa Harcourt knows she can never be anything
more than *The de Rochemont Mistress*.

But Alexa—the one woman Guy wants—is also
the one woman whose reputation
forbids him to take her as his wife….

**Available from Harlequin Presents
December 2010**

REQUEST YOUR FREE BOOKS!

2 FREE NOVELS PLUS 2 FREE GIFTS!

HARLEQUIN®

Blaze™

Red-hot reads!

YES! Please send me 2 FREE Harlequin® Blaze™ novels and my 2 FREE gifts (gifts are worth about $10). After receiving them, if I don't wish to receive any more books, I can return the shipping statement marked "cancel." If I don't cancel, I will receive 6 brand-new novels every month and be billed just $4.24 per book in the U.S. or $4.71 per book in Canada. That's a saving of at least 15% off the cover price. It's quite a bargain. Shipping and handling is just 50¢ per book.* I understand that accepting the 2 free books and gifts places me under no obligation to buy anything. I can always return a shipment and cancel at any time. Even if I never buy another book, the two free books and gifts are mine to keep forever.

151/351 HDN E5LS

Name _____ (PLEASE PRINT)

Address _____ Apt. #

City _____ State/Prov. _____ Zip/Postal Code

Signature (if under 18, a parent or guardian must sign)

Mail to the **Harlequin Reader Service:**
IN U.S.A.: P.O. Box 1867, Buffalo, NY 14240-1867
IN CANADA: P.O. Box 609, Fort Erie, Ontario L2A 5X3

Not valid for current subscribers to Harlequin Blaze books.

Want to try two free books from another line?
Call 1-800-873-8635 or visit www.morefreebooks.com.

* Terms and prices subject to change without notice. Prices do not include applicable taxes. N.Y. residents add applicable sales tax. Canadian residents will be charged applicable provincial taxes and GST. Offer not valid in Quebec. This offer is limited to one order per household. All orders subject to approval. Credit or debit balances in a customer's account(s) may be offset by any other outstanding balance owed by or to the customer. Please allow 4 to 6 weeks for delivery. Offer available while quantities last.

Your Privacy: Harlequin Books is committed to protecting your privacy. Our Privacy Policy is available online at www.eHarlequin.com or upon request from the Reader Service. From time to time we make our lists of customers available to reputable third parties who may have a product or service of interest to you. If you would prefer we not share your name and address, please check here. ☐

Help us get it right—We strive for accurate, respectful and relevant communications. To clarify or modify your communication preferences, visit us at www.ReaderService.com/consumerschoice.

HB10R

COMING NEXT MONTH

Available November 30, 2010